The Secret of the Legendary Tribe

THE SECRET OF THE LEGENDARY TRIBE

John Roche

BELLE ISLE BOOKS
www.belleislebooks.com

ISBN: 978-1-953021-79-3
LCCN: 2022912179

Cover art by Maryia Kapitsa

Printed in the United States of America

Published by
Belle Isle Books (an imprint of Brandylane Publishers, Inc.)
5 S. 1st Street
Richmond, Virginia 23219

BELLE ISLE BOOKS
www.belleislebooks.com

belleislebooks.com | brandylanepublishers.com

For kids facing challenges, with hope this story reflects their good humor and strength.

Some people can find adventure in the simplest things. A trip to the grocery store in the family car is a high-speed chase in the mind of one person, while an afternoon at the neighborhood pool is a journey to the bottom of the sea in the imagination of another. But some people have a knack for finding real adventure. The Mahood and Gonzales kids fall into that category, and they would never forget their adventure that began in the Mahoods' backyard on a muggy July afternoon in Alexandria, Virginia.

"Hector, I'm not sure this is such a good idea," eleven-year-old Archie said as he wrung his little hands, adjusted his dark sunglasses, and tried to ignore the beads of sweat that were beginning to dot his forehead.

"Don't be silly." Hector grinned ear to ear and put his hand on Archie's shoulder. "I thought of it, Kay designed it, and you and Marci built it! How could anything possibly go wrong?"

"I don't know." Archie patted the grass by his feet until he found his sister Kay's toolbelt, then used her screwdriver to tighten the screws on the flying machine for the hundredth time, tracing them with his thumbs to be sure he hadn't missed any. Archie had been blind ever since he contracted a rare illness as an infant, so his other senses were heightened, and he could tell just by touching the device that it was sturdy, but whether it would fly was another story.

Hector ran his hand along the taut rope that connected the vehicle to a distant tree branch. He turned to Kay and proclaimed, "This thing's as safe as it gets!"

Kay wasn't listening; she was busily tapping the keys on her calculator and methodically recording her tabulations in her thick notebook. Kay, who was twelve years old, had decided that she was going to be an engineer when she grew up, so she was almost never without her calculator, graph paper notebook, and tool belt. Her autism made it challenging for her to interact with others, but she felt it also made it easier for her to concentrate on the mathematical calculations that always seemed to be flying through her head.

"Well, Kay, don't you agree? Tell Archie it's safe," Hector said.

Kay blew her long, dark hair out of her eyes and repeatedly snapped her fingers as she looked at her notebook. Kay fidgeted a lot, especially when she was concentrating hard on something. Hector had asked about it once, and Kay had explained that it was called "stimming," or self-stimulatory behavior, which some autistic people do. Hector now understood that snapping her fingers helped Kay keep calm and focus. After a long pause, she turned to Hector and said, "Yeah, I think it'll hold."

"See! I told you it'll work!" Hector beamed.

Archie took no notice of Hector's proclamation as he continued tightening the screws.

While Kay calculated and Archie fretted and Hector crowed, Hector's eleven-year-old sister, Marci, sat in her wheelchair with the family mutt, Smokey, in her lap. She was rubbing Smokey's belly excitedly in eager anticipation of what they were about to do.

Up to now, the summer had been pretty forgettable. In June, each of them had spent several weeks together at a day camp. That had been followed by the annual Mahood-Gonzales trip to Bethany Beach, Delaware, over the Fourth of July. Now they were just trying to savor every last day of summer before the dreaded return of the school year.

The Mahood and Gonzales families were neighbors. Kay and Archie were the only children of Michael and Mary Mahood. The Mahoods lived across the street from Richard and Linda Gonzales and their two children, Hector and Marci, who were twelve and eleven, just like the Mahood kids. The kids were the closest of friends, and it was rare to see one without the other three.

They were now immersed in their latest—and most important—project of the summer: building a new fort. At the beginning of the summer, they had built a fantastic fort in the woods behind the Mahoods' house, and it had been the envy of all the children in the surrounding neighborhoods. It had been made from sticks, old sheets taken from their families' linen closets, and various bits of junk they'd scavenged from the forest and their neighbors' trash cans. To the eyes of an adult, the fort had looked like a jumbled pile of garbage, but in the eyes of a child, it had been finer than the world's most elegant castle.

In fact, it may have been built a little too well, because the three Lucas brothers, the nastiest kids in town, had liked the fort so much that they'd demanded it for themselves. When the Mahood and Gonzalez kids had refused to give it to them, the Lucas brothers had returned to the fort that night and destroyed it. They'd broken every stick, torn every sheet, and trampled every piece of meticulously placed trash.

It was this outrage that had led the Mahood and Gonzales kids to hatch their latest plan. They would build another fort, but they would do it in a place where no one, not even the Lucas brothers, could destroy it.

Marci had suggested building it near a police station so the Lucas brothers would be afraid to pass by. This had sounded like a good idea at first, but everyone agreed that the point of any good fort was to make sure it was as far away as possible from all adults, so the police station was ruled out.

Next, Archie had suggested they build the fort in the low-lying branches of a tree and use a ladder to climb up. But this was also ruled out, because if it was low enough to be accessed by a ladder, then there would be no way to prevent the Lucas brothers from entering.

Finally, Hector had announced where they would build their next fort: in the high branches of one of the one-hundred-foot-tall black oaks that dominated the woods behind the Mahood house.

It was a perfect plan, except for two major problems. First, it would be difficult for them to build anything that high. Second, even if they could find a way to build it, a fort that high would be almost impossible for anyone to get to—especially Marci, who had been in a wheelchair most of her life due to a condition that left her legs underdeveloped.

That's where the Tree Flyer came in.

To ensure that no one but the Mahood and Gonzales kids could access the fort, Hector decided they would build a rope swing that could be taken down and put back up each day.

It would be no problem for Marci, who, despite her legs not being strong, had the upper body strength of someone twice her age. Hector entrusted Kay with its design, and after many hours of thought and various sketches, Kay had the final plans ready for the Tree Flyer.

The Tree Flyer was ingenious in its simplicity, consisting of just four simple parts: a long series of ropes tied together, a stone, a stake, and an old seat from a swing set. The first step in the Tree Flyer's construction was to tie one end of the rope to the stone. The second step was to use the stake to secure the other end of the rope in the ground at the base of the Black Oak. The third step was for Hector to stand at the base of the Black Oak and throw the stone over a large limb of an adjacent tree. The stone and the rope would then pass over the limb and land in the Mahoods' backyard. The fourth step was to remove the stone from the rope so they could use Kay's tools to replace it with the seat from the Gonzales's old swing set. The final step would be for one of the children to give it a test run and use the Tree Flyer to reach the higher branches of the oak. Naturally, the one to test it would be the bravest among them: Marci.

"Now Marci," Archie said, "you don't have to do this."

"She knows," Hector said as he slapped their father's old high school football helmet on Marci's head, buckled the chin strap, and lifted her out of her wheelchair.

Archie had his first-aid kit out and was taking an inventory of his bandages and gauze in case anything went wrong. When he was satisfied that he had all the necessary supplies, he approached Marci and grasped her wrist as Hector placed her in the Tree Flyer.

After a few moments, Archie said to Marci, "Your heart

rate is a little fast, but nothing to be worried about. How do you feel?"

"Great!" Marci exclaimed. "Never better!"

"Remember," Kay said as she closed her notebook and put her calculator in her pocket, "after we push you off the hill, you have to lean your head back to create as little wind resistance as possible."

"I know, I know," Marci said.

"You're absolutely sure you want to do this?" Archie asked again.

"Yup!" Marci replied. "Let's light this candle!"

They each grabbed a part of the swing and began slowly walking backward until the swing was pulled back to about shoulder height on Hector and Kay, and slightly over Archie's head.

"Ready, Marci?" Hector yelled.

"Ready!" Marci yelled back.

"Okay, on three: one, two, three!"

The three children rushed forward as fast as they could until the arc of Marci's swing had brought her back to ground level. As Hector, Kay, and Archie reached the precipice of the hill, they gave Marci one last thrust and each of them fell to the ground as Marci took off.

They watched in wonder as Marci glided off the hill into the empty space between the hilltop and the tree branches.

"Yee-haw!" Marci screamed in delight. She soared over the chasm that lay between the hill and the trunk of the giant oak. She flew toward the oak's limbs, about thirty feet above the forest floor.

The children standing back on the hilltop began to cheer. They cheered, "The Tree Flyer works! It actually works!"

As the Tree Flyer began its steep arc upward, Marci could practically see herself landing amidst the tree's branches. She began to brace herself to grab one of them when she heard an ominous sound—*CRACK!*

Everyone, including Smokey, looked up to see that the branch supporting the Tree Flyer was snapping in half.

Marci murmured, "That's not good."

For a moment, Marci seemed to hang suspended in the air. Each of the children watched from atop the hill, their jaws wide open. Soon enough, gravity took over and Marci plunged toward the forest floor.

"Ow!" came Marci's shrill cry as she crashed to the ground.

The children and Smokey raced down the hill. Even though Archie couldn't see, he knew every inch of the woods behind his house and reached Marci first.

"Are you alright?" he screamed as he arrived at Marci's side.

"It hurts! It hurts!" Marci cried. She was clutching her arm as she lay on her side on the forest floor. Dirt and dead leaves were jammed in the face mask of the football helmet.

"What hurts?" Hector asked.

"My arm," Marci moaned.

"Alright," Hector said, "let's get her out of the swing and get that helmet off."

They pulled Marci from the wreckage and lay her in a pile of leaves as she continued to moan.

Archie began to administer first aid by gently cleaning the cuts on Marci's injured arm while Kay knelt by Marci's side. Kay wanted to say something comforting to her friend, but she couldn't find the words, so she clasped her hand and tried to smile reassuringly.

Hector gulped and said, "I'm going to go tell Sofia about

this right now and call 9-1-1." Sofia was the Gonzales's nanny, and she was going to be seriously unhappy when Hector told her what happened. Hector sprinted off at full speed to give her the unwelcome news.

"Marci, I think your arm might be broken," Archie said.

Marci groaned as she looked up at the top of the big oak and scowled. "I almost made it," she said.

"Yeah," Kay replied, "you were almost there."

"It's a good thing you had that helmet on," Archie said. "I bet it saved your life."

"Next time we just need to find a bigger branch," Marci said.

"Next time!" Archie exclaimed. "What do you mean 'next time'?"

"We can't quit!" Marci replied.

"You could have died!" Archie said.

"Aw, don't be so dramatic," Marci said as she scratched Smokey behind the ears with her good arm.

A few moments later, an ambulance siren blared nearby, and the vehicle soon turned the corner. At the same time, Sofia emerged in a panic from the Gonzales's house across the street.

The Mahoods' babysitter, Joseph, also came out their front door with a yawn. Clearly, he had been napping, but even he could not sleep through the wail of the approaching ambulance. As the ambulance pulled up to the Mahoods' house, Kay explained to Joseph what had happened while Hector tried to calm Sofia down.

Two medics emerged from the ambulance with a stretcher. After getting directions from Hector, they hurried into the woods behind the Mahoods' house. When they arrived at Marci's side, Archie began explaining what he had done to stabilize her arm.

"Jeez, kid," said one of the medics, "have you been to medical school?"

"Not yet," Archie said with a smile.

The medics stabilized Marci's arm further and then loaded her onto the stretcher so they could carry her up to the ambulance.

"Well," a medic said to Archie after Marci was safely in the ambulance, "we usually have a friend or family member join us in the ambulance to keep the patient company—would you like to do it?"

Archie turned to Sofia and asked, "Can I?"

Sofia's eyes were wide and glassy as she opened her mouth, but nothing came out. She was flushed and having difficulty catching her breath. She had grown accustomed to the children getting into trouble on an almost-daily basis, but so far, she had managed to avoid any trips to the emergency room.

Sofia stood in silence for a moment before Hector realized she wasn't able to speak and piped in himself. "Yeah, Archie, you should go with them. The rest of us will follow in Sofia's car." Turning to Sofia, he said, "You're okay to drive us to the hospital, right?"

Sofia still had not emerged from her shocked state, so Hector repeated the question. Finally, after Hector asked a third time, Sofia answered, "Yes, of course. The rest of you can come in my car."

"Alright!" Archie exclaimed as he climbed into the back of the ambulance. "Can I use the electro-shockers?"

"Electro-shockers?" asked one of the medics. "I think you mean the defibrillator. I doubt we'll need to use that on this kid's arm, but maybe after we get to the hospital, I can show you how they work."

"Cool!" Archie said as he leapt up and down in the back of the ambulance.

Hector knelt down and patted Marci on her non-injured shoulder. "They're going to take good care of you, and Archie will be with you the whole time, so you've got nothing to worry about. The rest of us will be right behind you, okay?"

"Okay," Marci replied without a hint of fear in her voice. However, on the inside, she was actually beginning to get a little nervous as the pain in her arm grew worse.

"Take good care of her, Archie," Hector said.

"I will," Archie replied.

Then, as the back door to the ambulance began to shut, Marci called out, "Good luck talking to Dad!"

Hector waved goodbye and tried to keep a brave face. He knew it would fall to him to explain everything to his parents. It would be no easy task, but if there was one thing Hector did well, it was talk. He just hoped that Dr. Gonzales and Judge Gonzales—otherwise known as Mom and Dad—were in a mood to hear what he had to say. Of all the speeches he had made to bail himself and his friends out of a jam, this one would have to be his finest performance.

2

Hector, Kay, and Archie sat in a row of seats along the wall in the emergency room at Alexandria Hospital. Joseph sat a few chairs down from them, sleeping as usual, while Sofia had been allowed to join Marci and speak with the doctor.

The other children were nervous and waited anxiously for their parents to arrive. Every time the door to the emergency room swung open, their heads snapped in that direction. They were relieved each time they saw an unfamiliar face or heard the soft *pad, pad, pad* of the doctors' and nurses' sneakers on the hard tile floor. They knew that when their parents arrived, they would hear the ominous *click, clack, click* of their hard-soled shoes.

Hector had been mentally preparing his speech ever since the ambulance had driven away from his house, and he was beginning to think he had it down pat when he heard the sound they had all been dreading: *click, clack, click*.

As the children turned their heads to the door, they saw Mr. and Mrs. Mahood pass through with their jaws set and their brows furrowed. Dr. Gonzales followed right behind them, bearing a very similar look. Hector could see that someone was holding the door open for the other three adults, and he didn't need any help figuring out who it was. The same hand that was holding the door open was also the same hand that had first shown him how to grip a baseball bat and hold a pencil—it was Judge Gonzales, his father.

Judge Gonzales passed through the door after the other three adults. Hector and the others had expected him to have the most upset look of all, but he didn't. Instead he bore the same calm yet serious expression that he always seemed to wear, whether he was happy, sad, or indifferent.

At formal events, he was always introduced as the Honorable Richard Santos Gonzales, but to most everyone else in Alexandria, he was known simply as "the Judge." He was regarded as the wisest and fairest judge in the city, and his children knew him to be the same at home, but he was no softy. Hector and Marci also knew that when they made a mistake, there would be a price to pay.

As the Judge made his way down the hall—*click, clack, click*—Hector tried to gauge what kind of day it had been. Because the Judge's facial expression almost never changed, Hector and Marci had learned to pick up on other subtle cues in their father's mannerisms to get a read on what kind of mood he was really in.

As the Judge made his way down the corridor, holding his wife's hand, he took his glasses off with his free hand, pinched the bridge of his nose, and exhaled deeply. Hector swallowed hard, for he knew that this could mean only one thing—the Judge must have had a bad day. Hector knew the nose pinch and the exhale was about as bad as it could get.

"Oh no," Hector said aloud, "rough day in court."

Archie leaned over and whispered, "Good luck."

The moment Hector had been dreading had finally come. Somehow, he had to explain to his mother and father what on Earth they had been thinking, without getting them all grounded for the rest of the summer. He had his work cut out for him.

Dr. Gonzales went to the front desk, while the Judge and the Mahoods came over to where the children were sitting.

Hector had hoped to defuse some of the tension by making a joke, but before he could open his mouth, Mrs. Mahood snapped, "Joseph! Wake up!"

Joseph jumped out of his seat as though it was electrified and stood at attention before Mr. and Mrs. Mahood.

"What do you have to say for yourself?" Mrs. Mahood said, her arms crossed and her shoe tapping rapidly on the tile floor. "Were you asleep when Marci hurt herself in our back yard?"

Joseph stood with his mouth agape for what seemed like an eternity. The children were equally shocked. It hadn't occurred to them that their parents might be angrier at Joseph and Sofia than at them.

"Well?" Mrs. Mahood said in an accusatory tone. Mrs. Mahood was a Secret Service agent, and when she fixed her gaze on someone, she knew how to get their attention.

"It's okay, Mary," the Judge said. "This isn't Joseph's fault." Hector took no comfort from the fact that the Judge set his gaze squarely on him when he spoke those words.

Luckily, at that moment Dr. Gonzales came up and said to the Judge, "They said we can go back and see her. They just put the cast on her arm."

"We'll get out of your hair," Mr. Mahood said. "I can't tell you how sorry I am about this."

"Really, Mike, don't be sorry. Our kids know better than to

do this sort of thing," the Judge replied, glancing sideways at Hector.

"All the same, call us later to give us an update on Marci, and let us know if there's anything we can do."

"We certainly will," Dr. Gonzales said.

Kay and Archie rose out of their seats to leave with their parents. As they did so, they both mouthed the words, "Good luck," to Hector.

As the Mahoods left the hospital, the Judge looked down at Hector and said, "Come on, let's go see your sister."

When they entered Marci's hospital room, she was all smiles.

"Hey everybody!" she exclaimed as they entered the room. "Isn't this thing awesome?" She pointed to the cast on her arm.

Dr. Gonzales rushed to her and kissed her forehead. "Are you alright, sweetie?" she asked.

"Aw, yeah," Marci replied as she wiped the lipstick from her forehead with her uninjured arm. "Anybody got a pen? I want you guys to sign my cast."

"We'll get to that later," the Judge said. "Is there anything you need?"

"Nope," Marci replied. Then after a moment's hesitation, she said, "Well, I guess I'd like to know how long we're going to be grounded for so I know how long I have to wait to fly the Tree Flyer again."

"What was that?" Dr. Gonzales asked.

The Judge arched his eyebrow as he looked down at Hector.

"Well, son," he began, "that raises some interesting questions. First, what is the Tree Flyer? Second, how long *should* we ground you for?"

Hector's moment had come. He rose to his feet and clasped

his hands behind his back, as he had seen the lawyers do when he and Marci had visited his father's courtroom earlier that summer. Then, with an earnest look on his face, he began.

"Well, Dad," he said, "all I have to say is how proud I am of Marci and the other kids."

"Are you proud that your sister broke her arm?" his mother asked, her arms folded sternly across her chest.

"No, Mom," he continued, "I'm proud of everyone—especially Marci—because of their courage. The courage they showed in building the Tree Flyer and sending her on her maiden voyage is the same courage the Wright Brothers showed when they took their first flight at Kitty Hawk. It's the same courage Sally Ride showed when she became the first American woman in space. And it's the same courage this country will need to conquer the next frontiers."

Based on the frowns on his parents' faces, Hector could tell his argument wasn't working, but he took another stab.

"By golly," he continued, "what Marci and us did today just makes me so proud to be an American!"

The Judge clenched and unclenched his jaw a few times before saying, "Son, we're not here to listen to a campaign speech. Do you have an explanation or not?"

It didn't take a genius to realize that Hector's first argument had only angered them. It was time to change tactics.

"Well, Mom and Dad," he said with a laugh, "I'm not really sure what you're so angry about. I mean, if you think about it, Marci could have died falling from that height. We should really be celebrating that she's only got a broken arm!"

"Hector Santos Gonzales, I'm beginning to run out of patience," Dr. Gonzales replied.

"I just think you should look on the bright side, that's all,"

Hector continued. "You're the one who's always telling us to look at the glass as half full, and I would say that what happened today makes the glass more than half full. Marci stared death straight in the face and came away with just a few bumps and bruises!"

The Judge exhaled deeply and said, "Alright, I've heard just about enough. Let's get home so your mother and I can decide how long to ground you for this nonsense."

Hector knew this was probably going to end with him having to accept responsibility for what had happened, but he thought he would try playing one last card: the sympathy card.

"Okay," Hector replied as he cast his gaze to the floor. "I guess you're right. I suppose we'll just have to accept what the Lucas boys did to us."

"What did the Lucas boys do now?" Dr. Gonzales asked with genuine concern in her voice.

Aha, Hector thought, *finally, an argument that has grabbed Mom's attention!* As the best pediatric surgeon in the area, Dr. Gonzales had mended and stitched many a child whose injuries were attributable to something the Lucas boys had done, so she knew them all too well.

"Well, Mom," Hector began, "as you know, we've had a tense relationship with the Lucas boys. As I think you're also aware, last week we built a wonderful fort down in the woods behind—"

"Yes, I know all about the fort, Hector," his mother broke in. "Each of you ruined a new outfit last week digging in all that mud."

Hector held his palms to the sky in befuddlement. "How are we supposed to make a decent fort without using mud?

It's the next best thing to concrete, and we don't exactly have the money for concrete."

Dr. Gonzales looked unamused, so Hector quickly moved on.

"Anyway, we spent several days constructing what I think was one of the finest forts ever built in Alexandria. Then, when we went to make some additions to the fort this past Monday, who do we find sitting there but the Lucas boys."

"And they were smoking!" Marci added.

"That's right," Hector continued, "Snake and Butch Lucas were smoking while their brother Dirk was chewing tobacco. Even so, in spite of their filthy habits and surly attitude, we tried to be nice to them."

"We really did, Mom," Marci said. "We even asked if they wanted to help us build the fort."

Hector shook his head in dismay. "Yes, we did try to play nice with them, but as you can imagine, they had other ideas. They told us we had to give them the fort. When we refused, they told us we'd be sorry. So, we went home that night after putting the finishing touches on our fort, and when we returned the next day, the entire thing had been destroyed and someone had spray painted the words, 'WE SED YOOD BE SORY.' Of course, almost every word was misspelled, which told us without a doubt who the culprits were."

At this point, Judge Gonzales broke in. "So, you built the Tree Flyer so you could build a fort so high up in the trees that the Lucas boys wouldn't be able to reach it."

"Exactly! The idea for the Tree Flyer was mine, but Kay designed it, Archie built it, and Marci was going to fly it."

"Whaddaya mean 'was going to fly it'?" Marci said as she sat up in her hospital bed. "I *did* fly it."

"Be careful, Marci." Dr. Gonzales rushed over to Marci's bed and gently lowered her back into her pillows. "You can't make quick movements like that with your cast on."

"But I *did* fly it," she persisted. "I just had some trouble with the landing."

"Children," Judge Gonzales said, "this Tree Flyer sounds like a really foolish idea, but I will say your mother and I are very proud of you for not retaliating against the Lucas boys *this time*."

By "this time," the Judge was referring to an incident the previous winter when the children had devised a catapult that could launch ten-pound snowballs twenty yards. The catapult had been built in defense of an ice fortress they'd created after a massive blizzard. The children knew the Lucas boys would try and destroy the fortress, so they built the catapult to ward them off when they arrived. Unfortunately, when one of the Lucas boys got a black eye from a snowball, Mrs. Lucas had placed a call to the Alexandria sheriff. That had resulted in a front-page story the next day in the *Alexandria Gazette* about how the sheriff had forced Judge Gonzales's children to dismantle a deadly weapon they had constructed in their front yard. Needless to say, the Judge had not been amused.

The Judge continued, "But instead of trying to build a fort high up in the trees where you were bound to hurt yourselves, you should have come to your mother and me and simply told us what the Lucas boys were doing."

Hector and Marci rolled their eyes at this bit of advice, which frustrated Dr. Gonzales to no end.

"I do not want to hear any nonsense about being tattletales. There are times when you need to tell your parents what's going on. If the Lucas boys or anyone else is bullying you, we need to know about it so we can deal with their parents."

Hector was getting frustrated, mostly because his arguments were clearly having no effect on his parents. Unfortunately, his frustration got the better of him, and he began to make an argument that he regretted the moment the words left his lips.

"I don't know why you're blaming us for this," Hector began. "I mean, where was the adult supervision? Aren't you the people responsible for keeping us out of trouble? Has it ever occurred to you that maybe this is all your fault?"

The Judge and Dr. Gonzales didn't say a word, but Hector could tell from their pursed lips and furrowed brows they were not amused. Hector knew he had made a colossal mistake. The only thing to do now was damage control, because it was clear he was going to get grounded; the only question was for how long.

"Mom, Dad, I'm sorry for what we did."

"Yeah," Marci added begrudgingly. "The Tree Flyer was a bad idea. We should have had more sense."

A few tense moments of silence passed before the Judge said, "Well children, that should do for now. We can discuss your punishment when we get home."

Hector was glum as they left the hospital that night. He assumed he would be grounded for a few days with no playing outdoors, no TV, and no video games.

As it later turned out, the Judge and Dr. Gonzales grounded Hector for an unprecedented six weeks, partly due to his behavior at the hospital. Marci went unpunished because their parents determined that her broken arm and itchy cast were punishment enough.

Hector knew his punishment was well deserved, but he was still bitter that by the time he had served his full sentence, the summer would almost be over. Of course, at the time, he and Marci had no way of knowing that the end of the summer would change their lives forever.

The weeks that Hector spent indoors without television or video games felt like they would never end, but Marci was nice enough to keep him company as her arm healed. They passed the time together by reading some of the books in the Judge's home office. One of the books Marci enjoyed the most was about the history of Alexandria, Virginia, and she learned all sorts of interesting trivia about their hometown.

For instance, she learned that Alexandria had been named for the Scotsman John Alexander, who in 1669 had purchased the land that included the future site of Alexandria in exchange for six thousand pounds of tobacco. She also learned that in 1801, Virginia had given the city of Alexandria to the federal government so it could be part of the new capital city. In 1847, the federal government gave the city back to Virginia, but for forty-six years, Alexandria was just another neighborhood in Washington, DC.

But what captured Marci's imagination most was what she read about the George Washington Masonic Temple located at the very center of Alexandria. The Temple was a formidable, nine-story tower that stood atop the highest point in the city.

It had been built in 1910 by the Masons, a secretive group that counted George Washington and many other presidents among its former members. According to the history book, the Temple stored one of the world's largest collections of artifacts from early colonial days, most of which were donated to the Masons after President Washington died.

This had prompted Marci to search online for anything she could find about the Masons and the Temple, and some of the sites she'd come across had wild theories about what was really stored in the Temple. Most intriguing was one site that claimed there were ancient Native American artifacts stored in the Temple, but the Masons wouldn't confirm or deny those rumors. The public could tour the Temple during the day and even go up to the observation deck on the ninth floor to take in views of Washington, DC, the Potomac River, and miles of the surrounding area, but several floors in between were off-limits to the public. The site Marci had found theorized that the private floors of the Temple were used for secret rituals, but again, the Masons would not discuss what the floors were used for or why they were off limits. The notions of secret Native American artifacts and floors where private rituals took place were too cool for Marci to resist, so she showed the site to her brother.

"I bet the Mahoods would be interested to find out if there really are any Native American artifacts being stored in the Temple," Hector said.

"Yeah," Marci replied. "Kay told me it's a real problem that so many tribes have their history scattered around the world in different museums and private collections."

Mrs. Mahood and her children were members of the Patawomeck Tribe, which was based in Fredericksburg,

Virginia, just forty-five minutes south of Alexandria.

"Wouldn't it be great to explore the Temple and see if we could get to the bottom of this?" Hector mused.

"It would be nice to have an adventure that actually had a chance of accomplishing something other than just getting us into a bunch of trouble," Marci said with a wink.

The first day that Hector was free to leave the house again, he and Marci told Archie and Kay what they had read about the Temple. They were of course all familiar with the Temple. It was the most prominent building in Alexandria, and whenever it snowed, the Judge would drive them over so they could sled down the long, steep slopes that surrounded the Temple on all sides. The mysteries Hector and Marci mentioned made for a tantalizing end-of-summer adventure, and both Kay and Archie were keen to find out if there really were any Native American artifacts in the Temple so they could start campaigning to have those artifacts returned to their tribes. But even so, they weren't sure how they could actually pull off Hector's idea of biking to the Temple to investigate.

"Hector, you know we're not allowed to ride our bikes that far without an adult," Kay said.

"Yeah," Archie agreed, "that's like three miles outside the Box."

"The Box" was the area surrounding their neighborhood where the children were allowed to ride their bikes—or wheelchair, in Marci's case—without an adult. It consisted of a three-square-mile grid between Seminary Road, Howard Street, Duke Street, and Van Dorn Street. Since most of the streets within the Box were residential and had very light car traffic, their parents had decided the children could ride their bikes along them unattended. Patrick Henry Elementary School and

James K. Polk Elementary School were both located inside the Box, so the children had access to both school's ball fields and playgrounds.

Hector didn't have much to say in response. Kay and Archie were both right; the Temple was at least three miles outside the Box, maybe even more. Plus, given the trouble they had just gotten into with the Tree Flyer, they couldn't afford another screw-up.

Marci, on the other hand, knew once the school year started, there would be no opportunities for them to tackle this mystery until winter break at the earliest. And given some of the wild theories she had read online, she simply couldn't wait that long.

"Yeah, you guys are right." Marci rubbed her arm, as she was still getting used to having the cast off. "We probably shouldn't do it." Then she sighed heavily and enjoyed a nice, long, dramatic pause before saying, "I guess we'll never know if the Spearhead is really there."

Kay and Archie both stiffened as Marci picked up a Spiderman comic book and began to read.

"Did you say 'Spearhead'?" Archie asked.

Marci pretended not to hear him, yawning and turning the page of her comic book.

"Marci!" Kay said with agitation in her voice as she snapped her fingers furiously.

Marci looked up in feigned surprise. "I'm sorry, did you say something?"

"Did you say 'Spearhead'?" Archie repeated.

Marci didn't even look at them as she continued flipping the pages of her comic book. "Oh, it's not important," she replied. "The Temple's too far away, remember?"

"Come on," Kay implored. "This is *important*. Did you say 'Spearhead'?"

Marci could see Kay and Archie were genuinely worked up about this, so she closed the comic book and stopped being coy.

"Yeah, I said 'Spearhead.' Have you heard of it?"

"What did you read online about it?" Archie asked.

"Not much," Marci replied. "Just that some people believe there's a quartz spearhead among the artifacts in the Temple that holds great powers. It sounded pretty cool to me."

"I can't believe it," Archie said.

"Do you think it could be the Patawomeck Spearhead?" Kay asked her brother.

"Whoa, whoa, whoa," Hector broke in. "The Spearhead belongs to *your* tribe?"

Kay was clearly getting very uncomfortable with this discussion and began snapping her fingers faster than Marci and Hector had ever seen.

Archie took a deep breath and said, "The Spearhead is very important to our tribe." Then he went on to explain why.

The Patawomeck Tribe was one of Virginia's eleven recognized Native American tribes. "Potomac" was how the English spelled Patawomeck, and the Tribe had lived along the banks of the great river that bore their name for centuries. The Patawomeck had been part of the Powhatan Federation, which was a group of about thirty Algonquian tribes that lived in eastern Virginia when the English arrived in Virginia. The Patawomeck at first befriended the English, and their chief, Wahanganoche, was even issued a silver badge by the King of England to wear for safety when traveling among the English.

But in 1666, the General Council of Virginia declared war

on the Patawomeck so they could take their land. Descendants of the survivors of that war made up the current Patawomeck Tribe, including Mrs. Mahood and her children. "Kay" and "Archie" were actually nicknames for their full Patawomeck names, Ka-Okee and Archihu.

"Chief Wahanganoche carried a spear with a tip made out of quartz," Archie said. "It was believed to give him great power on the battlefield and even greater healing powers off it."

"But he died a few years before our tribe was massacred by the English, and his spear went missing," Kay added. "Legend has it that one of Chief Wahanganoche's daughters and her husband escaped with the quartz Spearhead after the massacre and took refuge on a small island in the Potomac near what would become George Washington's Mount Vernon estate."

"The family lived there for about two centuries and even provided a safe haven for slaves who managed to escape from the surrounding plantations," Archie said. "The island came to be known as Freedom Island."

"But when word eventually got out that the Spearhead still existed and was on Freedom Island, the family came under attack by mercenaries trying to get their hands on the Spearhead for its enormous value," Kay said. "The family was able to fend off the mercenaries, but the surviving members of the Tribe decided the only way to protect the family and the Spearhead was for them to leave Freedom Island. So that's what they did, but the Tribe kept secret where they went or what happened to the Spearhead. Its location remains a mystery to the public."

When Kay and Archie were done speaking, Hector and Marci stood there, awestruck, their mouths hanging open. They could not believe what they had just heard. Perhaps only a few miles from their home was a lost Patawomeck artifact rumored to possess great powers. Finding the Spearhead would be the greatest adventure of not only the summer, but their entire lives.

"So, does that mean you guys are willing to go to the Temple now?" Marci asked.

"I don't see how we have any choice," Archie replied. "The Spearhead belongs with our tribe, not in the Masonic Temple."

"Alright," Hector said, "then I guess we'll need a plan."

They spent the rest of the morning plotting their adventure. They decided they would probably need at least two trips to the Temple before they could get to the Spearhead. Since the Temple was nine stories high and had all kinds of secret rooms, it was unlikely they would be able to search the entire place in one day.

Phase one of the plan was to go one day and take a public tour. During the tour, one of them would slip away from the group, explore, and memorize the layout as much as possible. If they weren't able to find the Spearhead on the first day, they would go back a couple days later to continue the search.

On their second trip, they would bring Smokey and use him as a diversion to search through the rest of the Temple. The plan was to let Smokey loose in the main vestibule. As he ran around and caused a commotion, one or two of the kids would slip past the distracted guards and continue exploring the Temple. If they couldn't find the Spearhead after the second trip, they would have to put their heads together to decide what to do next.

"Guys, I think we've got a plan," Hector said in satisfaction. "Should we go to the Temple?"

"Alright!" Kay bolted out of their room and into the garage, where the tandem bike she rode with Archie awaited. After weeks of boredom, they were finally going to have some fun again!

Kay assumed her usual position at the front of the tandem bike with Archie in the rear, and Hector hopped on his bike. Marci flipped a lever on the side of her wheelchair that released two hand pedals, which she could use to make her chair go just as fast as any bike. The hand pedals were just one of the many gadgets Kay had added to Marci's wheelchair to make it one of the most sophisticated wheelchairs around.

Hector rode up front and led the group. Marci followed right behind him, with Kay and Archie in the rear. Smokey assumed his usual position running alongside Kay and Archie's bike.

As they took off a little before eleven o'clock that day, they each marveled at what a perfect morning it was. The sun was shining brightly, there wasn't a cloud in the sky, and the typical August humidity had even given way to a nice cool breeze. They couldn't have asked for a better day.

They rode down the steep hill on Kemper Street, turned left on Jordan Street, and rode uphill until they got to Seminary Road. When they reached the summit of the hill, they turned right onto Seminary and headed down to the corner of Howard Street, right in front of Alexandria Hospital.

They were now at the northwest corner of the Box. The only way for them to stay within its confines was to take a right on Howard. Of course, if they did that, they would never arrive at the Masonic Temple. In order to get to the Masonic Temple, they needed to cross Howard and keep heading down Seminary.

As the children bunched together at the corner and waited

for the crosswalk signal, they could feel one another's tension. None of them spoke.

Hector broke the silence. "No one has to do this. If you guys want to turn back, I promise I won't give you a hard time. I've gotten everyone in enough trouble to last a lifetime."

Kay looked at him. "Don't blame yourself for the Tree Flyer. Any one of us could have backed out if we thought it was a bad idea."

"Yeah," Marci agreed. "We made that decision together."

Archie, Marci, and Kay all nodded, which gave Hector some comfort, but he still had some doubts.

"Well, all the same," Hector replied, "I'll understand if you want to go back. If anyone is having second thoughts, just say the word, and we'll all head back."

There was a moment of silence before Marci broke in, "But you're chicken if you back out now."

Hector laughed at his younger sister, as did the others. As if on cue, the "walk" signal flashed across the street. Without another moment's hesitation, Hector rode into the crosswalk.

But he'd forgotten to make sure the road was clear. In a split second, their dream of one last great summer adventure took a terrible turn.

M arci sat in her wheelchair outside the operating room in a daze. Archie and Kay sat silently in the chairs along the wall, equally shocked by what had happened. The only other person in the hallway was the old man who had been driving the car that struck Hector. He had been speeding and trying to beat a red light as the crosswalk had turned. He was distraught.

The only fortunate thing about Hector's accident was that it had happened right outside Alexandria Hospital, so Kay and Archie were quickly able to grab some paramedics off the sidewalk to come help. Hector was immediately taken into surgery.

Marci had been with Hector from the moment after he'd been hit until the moment he was taken through the double doors. He had been breathing the entire time, but his eyes hadn't opened once.

Eventually Sofia and Joseph arrived. Joseph's face was drawn and haggard, like he had just awoken from a nightmare, and Sofia's eyes were moist and red from crying. Both of them hugged each of the children one by one and tried to reassure them.

A few moments later, Dr. Gonzales and the Judge arrived.

Dr. Gonzales was still wearing her surgical scrubs from the hospital in Washington, DC, where she worked, and the Judge still had on his black robe. They had each left work the instant they'd received the news.

The Judge and Dr. Gonzales knelt down on the floor in front of the children and hugged them close. The Judge then took a seat with the children while Dr. Gonzales tried to talk to a doctor or a nurse to find out what was happening. Eventually, Dr. Gonzales returned and asked the Judge to join her. They both walked off down a long hallway while the children and the nannies waited behind.

After an interminably long wait, the Judge returned alone.

"Hector is still in surgery," he said, his voice uncharacteristically weak. "They expect it will take at least a few more hours." As he finished speaking, he removed his eyeglasses and pinched the bridge of his nose, letting out a sigh.

Everyone sat in silence for a moment until Marci asked the question that was on all their minds. "Is he going to be alright?"

The Judge waited a moment before answering, "Yes, of course," but he wasn't very convincing.

They all sat in silence for another few moments until the Judge said, "I think everyone should probably go home now. Mom and I will stay here until Hector gets out." Then he looked at Sofia and said, "Do you think you would be able to spend the night at the house tonight?"

"Of course," she replied.

"But we want to stay until we know Hector's okay," Marci interjected.

"I know you all want to stay here," the Judge said, "but there's nothing any of us can do. Your mother and I will stay here, and as soon as we have any news, we'll call, I promise. In the meantime, I think the best thing is for all of you to go home and keep Hector in your thoughts."

Before getting into Sofia's car, Marci smiled weakly as Kay and Archie opened the doors to Joseph's car. Kay whispered, "Good luck."

Marci nodded her appreciation as Sofia started the car. In a few moments, they were all back home, where Marci went to her room and thought of nothing but her brother and how much she hoped the doctors could make him better. But, even as she did so, the first thoughts began to creep into her mind about what she, Kay, and Archie could do to help Hector themselves if the doctors couldn't.

W hen the Judge finally came home that night, he looked tired and crestfallen. He was momentarily taken aback when he opened the door and saw Marci, Sofia, and Smokey waiting for him in the kitchen. He tried to force a wan smile, but it was no use.

"Hello everyone," he said softly as he closed the door behind him. "I didn't expect you to still be up."

No one said a word as they waited for him to answer the question that was on all their minds.

The Judge sighed heavily as he said, "Hector got out of surgery a couple hours ago, but he hasn't woken up yet."

No one quite knew what to make of this, including the Judge.

"What does that mean?" Marci asked.

The Judge paused for a moment before he said, "I don't know. They can't tell us much of anything now. All we know right now is that he's alive, so we've just got to be thankful for that."

"When does he come home?" Marci asked.

"Soon, I hope," the Judge said without a trace of hope in his voice. "We've just got to keep hoping for the best," he added as he walked past them into the hallway and began to take off his tie.

Marci and Sofia watched him as he lumbered into the kitchen and poured a glass of water. They slowly followed behind but said nothing.

After waiting a few moments to let the Judge finish his glass of water, Marci asked, "Where's Mom?"

"She's going to stay in Hector's room tonight," he replied. "I came home to relieve Sofia."

"I'm happy to stay the night, Judge Gonzales," Sofia said.

"That's very nice of you," the Judge replied, "but you should get home to your family. Thank you for everything you've done tonight."

"Okay," Sofia said, "then I will see you in the morning."

"Thank you," the Judge replied.

Sofia kissed Marci on the cheek and then left.

Marci sat in silence as the Judge sat at the table and slowly ran his fingers through his thinning brown hair. He had deep bags under his eyes, and his face was drawn as though something had been pulling on his cheeks all day.

Marci eventually broke the silence by asking, "Is there anything I can do to help?"

The Judge didn't say anything in response for a few seconds before letting out a deep sigh and saying, "All we can do is try to stay positive and think good thoughts for Hector. That's all we can do."

"Okay," Marci replied. "Then that's what I'll do. Goodnight, Dad."

"Good night," he murmured in response.

Marci found it nearly impossible to sleep that night, as the plan she had begun to hatch to save her brother raced through her mind. As sleep eventually claimed her, the last thing she told herself was that if the doctors were not able to save Hector, then she, Kay, and Archie would just have to do it themselves.

The next morning, Marci awoke early, but the Judge had already left for the hospital. When she made her way into the kitchen, she saw Sofia standing there cooking breakfast.

"Good morning," Sofia said. "Did you manage to get any sleep last night?"

"A little. Have you heard anything about Hector?" Marci asked.

"No, I'm sorry, honey," Sofia replied. "Your father didn't have any news when I saw him this morning."

"Is he at the hospital already?" Marci asked.

"Yes, he left just a few minutes ago," said Sofia. "He didn't want to wake you since you went to bed so late."

As Marci rolled up to the table and began to pile pancakes and bacon onto her plate, she asked, "Can we go to the hospital this morning?"

"Yes," Sofia replied, "right after you eat."

With that, Marci suddenly had incentive to scarf down her breakfast as quickly as possible. Once she'd done so, she dressed herself in no time at all and was sitting outside, waiting anxiously for Sofia to drive her to the hospital.

When they arrived at the hospital, they went directly to the information desk and asked where Hector's room was.

"Room 1305, in the intensive care unit," the nice old lady behind the desk told them.

As they made their way through the labyrinth of elevators and hallways to get to Room 1305, Marci looked up at Sofia and asked, "Is it bad that he's in the intensive care unit?"

"No, sweetie," Sofia replied. "It's a special place where all the best doctors work."

"Oh, that's good," Marci said, but she could tell from Sofia's voice that if Hector was in the intensive care unit, then he must be seriously hurt.

Upon entering Room 1305, Marci was struck by the number of tubes, gadgets, and gizmos that were hooked up to and surrounding Hector. The Judge and Dr. Gonzales were sitting beside the bed, holding hands. Dr. Gonzales had been at the end of a long shift at the hospital when she'd first received the news about Hector, and after spending all night at Hector's bedside, she had not slept in about two days. The Judge had pleaded with her to go home the night before, but she'd refused to leave. Marci had never seen her look so tired.

"Marci," Dr. Gonzales said with a forced smile as Marci and Sofia entered. She held out her arms, and Marci rolled her wheelchair over so she could hug her mother.

Neither of them said a word until Marci looked up from her mother's arms and asked, "Is Hector going to be okay?"

Dr. Gonzales looked at Marci for a long moment, then looked at the Judge and then back to Marci. Rather than answer Marci's question, she simply pulled her closer. At that moment, Marci truly understood that Hector was in real danger.

○○○

They spent the rest of the morning in the hospital room, silently watching Hector's chest heave up and down as the machines around him pumped and churned. Since Marci was adamant about staying at the hospital that day, Sofia had left to take care of Smokey back at the house. Around noon, Kay and Archie arrived with their mother and father. The Judge and Dr. Gonzales were delighted to see their old friends, and they went out in the hallway to talk for a moment without the children.

"Is he going to be alright?" Kay asked, snapping her fingers furiously with anxiety over Hector's condition.

"I don't know," Marci mumbled. "No one will give me a straight answer, which means it can't be good."

"Is there anything we can do?" Archie asked.

"No," Marci said, "you guys have gotten in enough trouble with us already this summer."

"What does that mean?" Archie asked. "If you've got something planned, we want in."

"No, you don't," Marci said. "I'm going to the Temple tonight, and I have to do it alone."

"You're doing what!" Kay exclaimed.

"Wait, I don't get it," Archie said. "Why are you going to the Temple?"

"To get something that will fix Hector," Marci said.

"What?" Archie asked.

"The Spearhead," Marci answered. "And I'll have a way easier time if I go alone, so you can just forget about coming with me."

"Oh no you don't," Kay broke in. "We're going too."

"You bet we are," Archie said. "It's our tribe's Spearhead, after all!"

"Auugh, you guys don't understand," Marci said. "We'll get caught if there are too many of us. I have to do this alone!"

"But what makes you think you'll even be able to get into the Temple in the middle of the night?" Archie asked.

"Guys!" Kay whispered between clenched teeth as she motioned toward the door. "They're coming back."

○○○

They passed the afternoon chatting around Hector's bedside. When the Mahoods left later that afternoon, Marci and her father went down to the hospital cafeteria to get some dinner and bring it back up to the room.

Once they were done with dinner, Marci stayed in the room for another or hour or so with her parents until the Judge decided it was time to go home. He implored Dr. Gonzales to go home with Marci, but she would not leave Hector's bedside. The Judge relented without putting up too much of a fight; he knew that when his wife had made up her mind up about something, there was not much point trying to convince her otherwise. Under normal circumstances, a visitor like Dr. Gonzales would not have been allowed to sleep overnight in the hospital, but since she had surgical privileges in Alexandria Hospital and knew every nurse and doctor in the building, an exception was made.

Before they left the hospital room, the Judge and Marci each kissed Hector on the cheek and wished him good night.

As Marci leaned in to kiss him, she whispered, "I'm going to fix everything tonight. Just hang on."

When Marci and the Judge arrived back at home, Smokey

met them at the door. When he saw that Hector was not with them, he let out a soft whimper.

"He'll be okay, boy," Marci said as she took Smokey in her lap.

As she lay in bed later that night, Marci began to have second thoughts about her plan to sneak out and ride to the Masonic Temple. She knew her father was consumed with worry about Hector, and the last thing he needed was her wheeling around Alexandria in the middle of the night. On the other hand, she could tell from her time at the hospital that day that she may be Hector's only hope. She had no choice.

Marci lay awake for another hour or so, until she heard the telltale footsteps of the Judge walking into his bathroom from his office that meant her father would be in bed soon. She heard water running as the Judge brushed his teeth, then tracked the sounds of his footsteps as he walked into his bedroom and crawled into bed.

Marci counted to a hundred to make sure the Judge was really down for the night, and then went into action. She had purposely left her clothes and shoes on so she wouldn't have to make a lot of noise putting them back on when she got out of bed. She slowly slid into her wheelchair, grabbed some money from her piggy bank just in case she needed it, and wheeled out into the kitchen. As she passed through the room, she glanced at the digital clock on the microwave, which indicated that it was one o'clock in the morning. As Marci took note of the time, she remembered that the Judge awoke every morning at six o'clock, no matter what. She would absolutely, positively have to be back in the house by then, or her goose was cooked.

"See ya in five hours," she said to no one in particular as she rolled out the back door into the backyard. As she wheeled herself onto the grass, she was startled by how bright the night was. She looked up at the sky and realized there was a full moon.

Marci made her way around to the side of the house, unlatched the gate, and pushed it open. But as she rolled through, she saw something that nearly gave her a heart attack.

"Oh my goodness!" Marci exclaimed as she spotted Kay and Archie standing on the other side of the gate in the moonlight with their tandem bike. "What do you guys think you're doing here?"

"We're coming with you," Archie replied.

"And someone else is too." Kay pointed behind Marci at Smokey, who had crept out of the house behind her.

"You've got to be kidding me," Marci said as she hung her head. "Even the dog won't let me do this alone."

"No, my friend," Archie replied with a wide grin, "we're not kidding at all."

"Just forget it." Marci threw up her hands and started wheeling her chair around. "There's no sense going with such a big group."

As she turned her chair around, she heard Archie say to Kay, "Then it looks like we'll have to do this ourselves."

"Wait, you guys can't go without me." Marci quickly wheeled back around.

"You bet we can," Archie replied. "If our tribe's Spearhead can save Hector, then we don't have a moment to lose."

"But we sure could use your help," Kay said.

Marci was annoyed by her friends' persistence, but she had to admit she was touched by how much they wanted to help her brother. And, of course, there was no way she could let them do this without her.

"So, have you guys given any thought to how we're going to get to the Temple?" Marci asked.

"We just figured we'd ride up Duke Street," Archie replied. "That's the straightest route."

"Yeah, but it's also the most well-lit," Marci replied. "Three kids and a dog traveling anywhere in the middle of the night is going to look awfully funny to any police officers out on patrol tonight, don't you think?"

"How else can we get there?" Kay asked.

Feeling like she was back in command, Marci said, "We need to go down Janney's Lane to King Street. That way's a lot darker, and there won't be nearly as many cars out. If we want to get there without drawing any attention to ourselves, that's the way to go."

"Okay," Archie said, "so what are we waiting for?"

With those words, Kay and Archie hopped on their bike, while Marci flipped the lever for the hand pedals on her wheelchair. They were each nervous but excited about a trip they hoped would lead them to something that would save Hector. They had no way of knowing that they were setting off on the first leg of an adventure that would change their lives forever.

7

The whole gang, including Smokey, made it to the Temple without incident. They passed one police car on Seminary Road just as they were riding past Episcopal High School, but thanks to some quick thinking by Kay, they scooted behind the old post office on the school grounds and weren't spotted. In just twenty minutes, they found themselves riding up the steep hill that led to the Temple.

Designed in the classical architecture of Greece and Rome, the nine-story Temple was capped with a small Egyptian pyramid. That evening, the 333-foot-tall building was bathed in moonlight, which somehow made it seem even taller as the kids rolled into the parking lot that sat atop Shooter's Hill, where the Temple stood. Marci had read that Shooter's Hill was where Thomas Jefferson had originally wanted to build the U.S. Capitol, but George Washington had nixed the idea because he thought it would be too controversial if the Capitol Building was placed in a city where he had so many business ties.

Surprisingly, a number of cars were parked in the Temple's parking lot despite the late hour.

"It looks like a lot of people are here," Kay informed Archie.

"I wonder what they're up to at this hour," Archie said.

"Well, with any luck we'll find out," Marci said. "Let's ride into the woods over there." She pointed to a wooded area that ringed the parking lot. As they pedaled over to the trees, she pulled another lever on her wheelchair that converted her tires into thick, off-road wheels that made it easier for her to roll across the grass into the woods.

As Archie and Kay lay their tandem bike down in the darkness and unstrapped their helmets, Marci asked the question that was on all their minds: "So, what do we do now?"

"Good question," Archie replied. "Anyone got any ideas?"

They each looked around in befuddlement. Even Smokey whimpered.

"I thought you had a plan," Kay said.

"Hey, you guys didn't have to come," Marci said with a smirk.

"Wait, I hear something," Archie said. Kay and Marci couldn't hear anything until a few seconds later, when they too heard the unmistakable sound of an approaching car. A wide grin spread across Marci's face as she watched a black Mercedes pull into the parking lot.

"Why are you looking at me like that?" Kay asked.

"Because I know how we're going to get into the Temple," she replied.

"How?" Archie asked.

"Kay, give me a lift," Marci said. She knew they were likely going to have to use the stairs in the Temple, so she'd have to leave her wheelchair behind.

Kay hoisted Marci onto her back the way she'd seen Hector do a thousand times before, and Marci latched on piggyback style.

"So what's your plan?" Kay asked.

Marci ignored her and said to Smokey, "Hey, boy. I need you to hold the door, okay?"

When Smokey was a puppy, Hector and Marci had trained him to hold doors for Marci, so he knew precisely what "hold the door" meant. He wagged his tail eagerly—all he needed now was for Marci to point him in the right direction.

As the door to the Mercedes opened, a man in a dark suit climbed out and quickly slammed it shut behind him. He then walked briskly toward the Temple, as though he was late for an appointment.

"What are we doing?" Archie whispered to Marci as they watched the man cross the parking lot.

"We're going to follow that guy into the Temple," Marci said. "We'll just need Smokey here to hold the door for us."

At that moment, the man in the dark suit reached the stairs leading up to the back door of the Temple. He took something out of his pocket and waved it past a panel on the door. A small green light flashed on the panel, and the door slowly opened. The man waited a moment, and then he walked in.

Marci then pointed at the door and said, "Okay, boy, go hold the door!"

Smokey didn't hesitate for a moment; he took off at top speed for the rear of the Temple. As he ran, the back door to the Temple started to close.

"He'll never make it," Kay said.

"Just watch," Marci replied.

"What if he gets stuck in the door?" Archie asked.

"We'll be just a few seconds behind him if that happens," Marci replied. "Let's go!"

With those words, Kay took off after Smokey with Marci

on her back. Archie raced behind them, clutching the back of Marci's shirt so he knew where to go.

Smokey had already covered about forty yards and was about to bound up the steps just as the door shut. He cleared all six steps in one leap and slid his slender body between the door and the frame moments before it closed. He whimpered ever so slightly, trapped between the door and frame, but luckily, the moment the automatic door felt resistance, it swung outward again.

"Oh, thank goodness," Kay said as she reached the steps.

"Good boy," Marci said as Smokey stood triumphantly in the doorway.

Kay stared into the doorway for a moment to see if she could catch a glimpse of what they were about to walk into, but the hallway beyond the door was too dark.

"So, are we gonna do this?" Marci asked.

"All for one and one for all, right?" Kay replied with a grin.

"Okay," Archie whispered, "let's do it."

With those words, Kay and Archie slowly tiptoed through the doorway with Marci still on Kay's back. As Smokey entered the building, the automatic door began to slowly close behind them.

Clickity, clickity, click. They all stopped in their tracks.

"What is that?" Marci hissed.

Kay and Archie looked down at their own feet to make sure they weren't causing the sound, but they each wore the same thing: rubber soled sneakers. That left only one culprit, and he most certainly wasn't wearing rubber soled sneakers or anything else on his feet.

"Smokey." Marci answered her own question and looked down at her poor dog. "His nails are too loud on this floor."

"He's gotta go back out," Archie said.

Smokey let out a quiet whimper but didn't put up a fight as Marci pointed at the door. He turned, looked at everyone with his moist eyes, and headed for the door.

"G'bye, boy," Marci said.

Archie walked with him and pushed the door open. As it swung outward and Smokey slowly slinked out, Archie said, "Stay nearby, boy, and be on the lookout for any trouble, okay?"

Smokey's ears perked up at the sound of those instructions. As long as he had a job to do, Smokey was happy. As the door began to shut, Smokey bounded down the steps and assumed a lookout post from the bushes alongside the Temple.

While the door closed, Archie turned back and walked toward the others in the dark hallway. All they had to guide their way were some burning torches that hung on the wall along either side of the hallway.

"I may not be able to see anything, but I can just tell this place is creepy," Archie said.

"Yeah," Marci replied. "Remember when we took that field trip here with our class last year? They didn't have these torches burning then."

"They must only use them at night," Kay said, before abruptly shutting her mouth.

The others didn't make a sound, or even breathe, as they suddenly heard something very ominous echoing through the hallway. The sound started softly but grew in strength like a slow wave.

"What is that?" Marci asked.

"It sounds like some sort of chant," Archie said.

The sound subsided again for a moment and then returned, slowly at first, then building in momentum and washing over them once more. Archie was right—it sounded like a men's chorus was warming up nearby.

"Let's go check it out," Marci said.

"Are you serious?" Kay gripped Marci's ankles tighter since she couldn't snap her fingers to alleviate her anxiety.

"We've already come this far," Marci whispered. "No sense turning back now."

Kay reluctantly started to creep down the marble hallway, her shadow dancing in the torchlight. Archie had his white cane folded up in his back pocket, but he opted not to use it since tapping it along the floor would have made too much noise. Instead, he continued to hold on to the back of Marci's shirt.

By the time they reached the end of the hallway, the chanting was much louder. It sounded as though it was coming from the floor directly above them. Much to Kay's relief, when she turned the corner, she saw nothing but an empty, square room in front of her with a large altar at the end. Along the wall of the room were eight massive granite columns, which appeared to support the entire building.

"Well, no one's down here," Kay said.

"What are the odds that the Spearhead is down here?" Archie asked.

"Not good," Marci replied. "This place is nine stories tall, and something tells me the Masons wouldn't put the Spearhead down here on this empty ground floor without anyone guarding it. Let's go see if the Spearhead is upstairs."

"Wait," Kay said, "shouldn't we at least look around this giant room to make sure the Spearhead isn't hidden down here?"

"Where do you think it's hidden?" Marci asked. "It's just a gigantic, empty room."

"I don't know," she replied. "Maybe there's a secret compartment behind one of those stones in the wall."

"Good luck finding it," Marci said. "The walls down here must have a thousand stones in them. How are you going to figure out which one it is?"

"I don't know," Kay said, "but what's your plan?"

"The plan is not to waste any time," Archie added. "If the Spearhead is hidden behind one of the stones, then we're out of luck because we don't have time to sit down here and search every one of them. I say we search the rest of the building and see if we can find some clues."

Kay reluctantly agreed, so she turned and headed over to the stone spiral staircase that led up to the main floor of the temple.

"You can put me down here," Marci said. "I can do the stairs on my own."

Kay put her down and watched as Marci led the way, quickly but silently pulling herself up the stone staircase with her powerful arms. Archie and Kay fell in line and crept silently after her. As they made their way, the chanting grew louder, and each of them grew increasingly nervous. Kay stuffed her hands in her pockets to keep herself from snapping her fingers.

They were each familiar with the main level of the Temple, since it was the area that was most readily accessible to the public via the majestic front entrance that looked out over Old Town Alexandria. Each of the children had been in the room a dozen times with their school classes or with visiting relatives over the years who asked to visit the mysterious building at the center of the city. The front entrance to the main level, with its large granite steps and tall columns, had been inspired by the Parthenon of Athens and provided a dramatic view of King Street and the train station below. Upon walking through the main gates, the first thing visitors noticed was the massive bronze statue of George Washington in the Masonic apron he'd worn when he'd laid the cornerstone at the U.S. Capitol in 1793. The rest of the hall was lined with tall pillars and murals of General Washington at different stages of his life.

As they neared the top of the stairs, the three friends slowly poked their heads over the top step. What they saw was odd to say the least: the spiral staircase had brought them to the northeast corner of the main hall, which put them at the end opposite the large statue. A room full of about sixty men sat facing the statue in rows of chairs, all chanting in its direction. They each wore long, hooded robes of white or gray that obscured their faces and bodies completely. Marci and Kay thought they looked like a group of monks gathered in prayer. Kay briefly described to Archie what they were looking at.

"What are they saying?" Marci whispered.

"It sounds like Latin," Kay replied. "But I don't know what it means."

A man wearing a bright red robe stood facing the congregation, leading the chanting. At his feet, three men knelt with their backs to the congregation. The man in the red robe would occasionally raise his head and look to the ceiling, but the children couldn't get a good glimpse of his face under the hood.

"It sounds pretty weird," Archie said.

"What's the point of this?" Kay asked.

"I'm guessing it's some sort of initiation ceremony," Marci said. "Those three guys kneeling up there are the only ones who aren't wearing a sash."

She was right. Each man, except the three who were kneeling, wore a sash of some kind over their robes. Some of the sashes appeared to be fairly plain, while others were quite colorful.

The children sat quietly peering out over the steps for a few minutes as the ceremony continued and the men ponderously droned their chants. Apparently they weren't the only ones who were bored by the proceedings, because one of the robed men in the back row had fallen asleep.

"That guy looks like he might fall out of his chair," Kay said.

"I can hear someone snoring," Archie said with a giggle.

"You know what else?" Marci added as she stared intently at the snoring man. "I think he just might be our ticket to the rest of the Temple."

"What do you mean?" Archie asked.

"He's got a ring of keys on his belt," Marci said.

Sure enough, hanging from the man's rope belt was a large ring of old-fashioned keys.

"What do you think we need keys for?" Kay asked.

"Well," Marci said, "we're not going to be able to search in this room for the Spearhead anytime soon, which means we're going to have to go up to the other floors and look for it. My guess is that every level of this place is locked up tight as a drum."

"This floor wasn't locked," Archie countered.

"You're right," Marci replied, "but there's also no door between this floor and the ground level, so there's nothing to lock. If I remember from the tour, all of the other floors have a door leading to them from this stairwell."

"That's right," Kay added. "And I'd bet my life each one of them is locked."

"So, you want to steal that guy's keys?" Archie asked.

"We won't *steal* them," Marci said. "We'll just *borrow* them. I'll be right back."

Before Kay and Archie could try to stop her, Marci began crawling commando-style across the floor. She looked like a frog with its legs splayed out as she made her way stealthily across the cold stones and crept closer and closer to the sleeping man.

As Marci finally got within a few inches of the snoring man's chair, Kay held her breath and described the scene to Archie in whispers. But, to their great relief, the man didn't move a muscle, even as Marci reached up, deftly untied his rope belt, and gingerly slipped the keys off. Kay and Archie expected the keys to jingle and jangle, but Marci was smart enough to grip the bunch together so they wouldn't move. When the keys were finally off the belt, she turned and continued her frog crawl back to the stairs.

When Marci finally got back to them, Archie said, "Good work. Now let's check this place out."

They slowly and quietly made their way up the stairs until they came to the first door in the stairwell. Marci carefully unfurled the keys in her hands and noticed they were embossed with various Masonic symbols. She balanced herself on her knees and selected the first key to try in the keyhole. The keys clanged together a bit, but they were barely audible over the drone of the chanting that was still going on downstairs.

"Nope." Marci withdrew the key from the hole after it failed to budge. Then she selected the next one and inserted it into the hole. There was still no movement.

"Not that one," she whispered.

There were twelve keys on the chain, so the children were

optimistic, even as each of the keys Marci inserted failed to work. But as the eighth and then the ninth key failed, their optimism began to fade.

Marci inserted the tenth key, but this time there was no resistance as it slid in easily. Without any effort, she turned the key, and they all heard a *click*.

"That's the one," Marci said with a toothy grin.

"I wonder what's in there," Kay said.

"Only one way to find out." Archie put his hand on the door and slowly pushed it open.

They each held their breath as the door swung open. To their great relief, what they found within was a nearly unfurnished room with no one inside.

"What is this place?" Kay asked as they entered.

The room they entered was actually quite similar to the stone room they'd entered on the ground floor. It was long and rectangular with a golden throne at the center of the far wall. Above the throne, the letters M.O.V.P.E.R. were inscribed in the stone wall. Aside from the throne and the strange letters above it, the room was completely empty.

Kay described the room to Archie, who asked, "Who's the throne for?"

"Beats me," Kay said. "I'm more interested in those letters. What does M.O.V.P.E.R. mean?"

"I think it stands for Mystic Order of Veiled Prophets of the Enchanted Realm," Archie said.

"And what makes you think that?" Marci asked.

"Because I heard them chanting that downstairs," he replied. "They were the only English words I heard them say the whole time we were down there."

"Well, now we know what those letters stand for, but we

still don't know where the Spearhead is," Kay said. "Let's go check out the next floor."

"Okay," Marci said as she jangled her keys, "let's go."

On the fourth floor, Marci was able to open the door with the third key she tried. What the children found on the other side of that door was vastly different from the room they had just left.

"Wow," was the only word that passed Marci and Kay's lips as they entered. The fourth floor of the Masonic Temple consisted of two grand levels connected by a long, wrought iron spiral staircase at one end. The whole space appeared to be some kind of mini museum dedicated to George Washington.

The first level housed exhibits depicting the different faces of Washington: plantation owner, soldier, and president.

"This place is awesome." Kay described it to Archie, who could tell from the sound of his sister's voice vibrating off the walls that it was a big room. "And there are braille placards on each exhibit," she added.

Kay put Marci on her back again as they entered the room and began looking around in amazement at the many intriguing artifacts, including a flag that had flown over Mount Vernon the day the President passed away and two military sabers that had been placed on Washington's coffin during his funeral.

On the second level, there were more displays related to the construction of the Temple, depictions of Masonic history, and various other objects from Mount Vernon and the Washington family.

"If I were going to hide the Spearhead somewhere, this would be a good place to do it," Marci said.

"Yeah," Kay replied, "we could spend the rest of the night in here and still be searching for it!"

"Remember, there are five other floors in this place," Archie added. "We've still got a lot of places to look if we don't find the Spearhead in here."

"Well, let's get started." Kay and Marci began searching the first level and Archie pulled out his cane and felt his way up to the second level.

After a while, Marci couldn't help but sigh in frustration. Unless they stumbled on something quickly, it was pretty clear to her that they would have a difficult time finding the Spearhead. *There's got to be some way to speed this up*, she thought. She tapped her index finger against her lips the same way the Judge did whenever he was pondering something. Then, as though he had been reading her mind, Archie called out from the upper level of the museum.

"Guys, I think you might want to come check this out. I think it's a clue."

Kay raced across the room to the spiral staircase with Marci on her back. As they reached Archie, they saw that he was running his fingers carefully along the edges of a large, old book that was propped open on a wooden stand.

"What is it?" Kay asked.

"It's the Washington family Bible," Archie replied, his hands running across the Braille sign mounted on the stand.

"Well, where's the clue?" Kay asked.

"Right there on the page," Archie replied.

Kay and Marci looked closer, but they couldn't see what Archie was talking about. The bible was open to the Book of Genesis, chapter thirteen, but as far as they could tell, there was nothing particularly unique about what they were looking at.

"I can tell that some of the letters on the page are underlined," Archie said as he ran his fingers across the page. "Can you tell me which ones?" The underlining on the page was barely visible to the naked eye, but Archie could clearly feel the indentations in the soft paper.

Marci read the letters out loud, and when she was done, Kay announced, "I think it makes some kind of riddle."

"What kind of riddle?" Archie asked.

"I'll be able to tell you in a bit." Kay put Marci down so she could jot the riddle in her notepad. Marci propped herself up on the rail before the bible and continued reading out the letters.

A couple minutes passed as Marci read aloud. Kay asked her to repeat a few of the letters, and when Marci was finally done, Kay simply crinkled up her nose.

"What's it say?" Marci asked Kay.

"It doesn't make much sense to me," Kay said, "but the underlined letters say: 'He who searches for the Patawomeck head of the spear need not look far, for the first piece is near. It rests among those relics that traveled with the great man when liberty stood in the valley and darkness was at hand. When the first piece is found, there is still yet another, but to find it, one must go where the Patawomeck lie next to their brothers. If the sojourner finds them, the spirit must be heard, for none other than she can reveal the third.'"

The three of them stood in silence for a moment before Marci said what was on all their minds: "What?"

"I don't know," Kay said as she concentrated on the words in her notepad. "It's pretty confusing."

"Alright, well let's break it down into pieces," Archie said. "The first line is, 'He who searches for the Patawomeck head of the spear need not look far, for the first piece is near.' That seems obvious enough: it must mean the first piece of the Spearhead is here in the Temple."

"But I don't get it," Marci replied. "I didn't know we were looking for pieces of the Spearhead. I thought we were looking for the entire thing."

"Yeah, it's strange, but that's what it says," Kay replied. "Now, the second line is, 'It rests among those relics that traveled with the great man when liberty stood in the valley and darkness was at hand.'"

"'The great man' must be George Washington, right?" Marci offered.

"That would be my guess," Kay replied. "And I'm guessing the 'relics that traveled' with him are right here in this museum, since it's full of old Washington relics."

"But what about the last part?" Archie asked. "What does 'when liberty stood in the valley and darkness was at hand,' mean?"

His question was met with silence, as none of them had the foggiest idea.

After a few moments, Kay began muttering to herself and snapping her fingers with her eyes closed: "Valley, valley, valley. Valley Forge!" Kay exclaimed. "That's what it means: Valley Forge! 'When liberty stood in the valley and darkness was at hand,' has to be a reference to the winter of 1778, which General Washington and the Continental Army spent at Valley Forge."

"What makes you think that?" Marci asked.

"That winter was miserable, and many of General Washington's soldiers died or deserted while the Continental Army camped out at Valley Forge to pass the long winter," Kay explained. "But when the weather finally broke, the army was so inspired by General Washington's leadership that winter that many people think *that* was when the tide turned and the colonists began to win the war."

"Alright," Archie said, "now we've just got to find an exhibit that has some of the old relics Washington had with him at Valley Forge."

With those words, they all scrambled about the museum in search of anything remotely relevant to Valley Forge. In order for Marci and Kay to cover more ground separately, Kay put Marci down so she could do her frog crawl about the room.

After several minutes, Marci said, "Well, I'm at a loss. We've searched every inch of this floor, and I haven't seen anything that says it's from Valley Forge."

"I think I can explain why," Kay called out from across the room.

"What do you mean?" Archie asked as he and Marci made their way across the room to see what Kay had found.

To Marci's dismay, Kay was standing in front of a blank space in the corner of the room. It appeared to have once housed part of an exhibit but was now completely empty.

"What's here?" Archie asked.

Above the empty space in the corner was a sign that read, General Washington's field trunk from Valley Forge is currently on loan to the National Museum of American History.

Kay read the sign aloud for Archie.

"Ugh," Archie said. "The American History Museum in Washington, DC?"

"Yup," Kay replied. "And that museum is guarded day and

night. There's no way we'll ever get our hands on General Washington's trunk if it's in that place."

"Man," Archie said, "I can't believe we did all this for nothing."

Marci listened and stroked her chin as an idea began to bubble its way up to the top of her brain.

"Do you have an idea?" Kay asked her. She had seen this pensive look on Marci's face a thousand times before and knew what it meant.

"Well," Marci began, "I think you guys are right that it's going to be tough to get real close to General Washington's field trunk during business hours at the museum."

"*Business hours?*" Kay repeated. "What other *hours* are we going to be able to get into the museum?"

"Well," Marci said, "maybe there's a way to go in *during* business hours but stay a little later than everyone else."

Archie was just about to ask her what she meant, but at that moment he noticed something very disturbing.

"Do you guys hear any more chanting?" he asked.

They each fell silent and barely breathed as they listened to hear if the Masons were still chanting downstairs. To their dismay, the chanting had stopped, only to be replaced by a more ominous sound.

"And do you guys hear those footsteps?" Archie asked.

At first Kay and Marci couldn't hear anything, but after a few more seconds, the sound of heavy footsteps reached them, lumbering in a slow, deliberate pace up the temple's stone stairs. Fear and panic washed over all of them.

"Come on." Kay picked up Marci and headed toward the door.

"Wait," Marci said. "There's nowhere to go but up. Even if

we outrun them, they might be going to the top floor. We'd be trapped."

"So what do we do?" Archie asked.

Marci looked over at one of the stained-glass windows.

"Does that window open?" she asked.

"What are you thinking of doing?" Archie asked.

Kay grabbed the latch on the window and held her breath for a moment before lifting it. To her surprise, the window swung open with ease. As she did so, the muggy August breeze blew in.

"Marci, are you completely nuts?" Archie asked.

Marci ignored the question, climbed off Kay's back, stuck her head out the window, and surveyed the ledge. It was narrow, but wide enough for them to go out without falling off—at least, she hoped so.

"Guys, this is the only way out without getting caught," she said.

Kay and Archie didn't know quite what to say. They could hear the footsteps in the stairwell drawing nearer, but they had no desire to climb out on a window ledge that was close to one hundred feet above the stony ground below.

"If we get caught, we'll never be able to get to General Washington's field trunk in time to help Hector," Marci implored them. "This is the only way."

Kay looked at Marci as though she had horns coming out of her head. Was she really suggesting that they climb out on this ledge?

But before Kay could think of an alternative escape route, Marci said, "Here goes nothin'." She pulled herself over the window ledge and crawled out. Once she was outside, she poked her head back in through the window and said with a grin, "Come on guys. It's nice out here."

"Well?" Archie asked, unable to tell just how crazy Marci's idea was without his sister's guidance.

"Alright," Kay said to Marci, "but if anything happens to one of us, you're gonna get it."

"That's the spirit," Marci responded cheerfully.

Marci and Kay helped guide Archie through the window. Once Archie was outside, Kay carefully, yet quickly as possible, climbed through the window herself. After pulling her foot through the window, she turned around and pulled the stained-glass pane closed behind her. As the window shut, she saw the door opening. Several large men ambled into the fourth-floor museum. The kids' greatest adventure was now in danger of ending before it could truly begin.

8

"Who's in here?" barked one of the Masons as he stormed into the room. His voice boomed so loud that Marci, Kay, and Archie could hear him from outside on the ledge.

"I don't think there's anybody in here," came the voice of another Mason.

"That's not what the motion sensor downstairs indicated," said the angry man. "And whoever's in here stole my keys. This door was definitely locked before."

"Nobody stole your keys," said another Mason. "You're always losing those things."

"Get lost," the angry Mason replied. "It can't be a coincidence that this door was definitely locked before, my keys are gone, and the motion sensor indicated movement in here!"

"They're in there looking for us," Kay whispered as she listened nervously outside the window, "and they know we took their keys." She shuffled her feet along the ledge and took her spot next to Archie.

As Kay spoke, the lights inside the museum went on. The kids held their breath each time one of the men inside walked past the window, sending a shadow dancing across the ledge.

Kay realized how lucky they were that it was a calm August night. If this had been a night when one of the DC area's notoriously windy summer thunderstorms was blowing through, they would barely have been able to stay on the ledge without falling to their doom.

Of course, not all of them were contemplating the danger of their situation. Marci was entranced by the view. To the east she could see Old Town Alexandria, the Potomac River in the distance, and the lights of a few cars crossing the Wilson Bridge into Maryland at this late hour. Then, by simply turning her head ninety degrees to the left, she could see all of Washington, DC, with the United States Capitol and the Washington Monument shining brightly.

"Wow," Marci said as she took in the breathtaking nighttime view. "How come we've never come out here before?"

"Because you're usually in a wheelchair and the rest of us have no interest in getting splattered on the ground," Archie replied. "It's times like this I don't mind being blind."

"*Shhhh!*" Kay quickly shushed them and glared at Marci. In an instant, Marci and Archie clammed up, suddenly less concerned about the mysterious men they were hiding from than what Kay had in store if they kept talking.

"Now, how can we get ourselves out of this?" Kay asked herself, suppressing the urge to snap her fingers to help her think.

About a minute had passed since they had clambered out on the ledge, but the lights were still on inside the museum and the occasional shadow flitting past the window indicated that the Masons were still in there searching for them. For all but Marci, it had been just about the longest minute of their lives.

They were each searching their minds for a way to get off

the ledge without falling to the limestone steps below—when Kay and Marci saw a most welcome sight: Smokey traipsing around the corner of the building and looking up at them.

Kay was worried that he was going to bark up at them and cause a ruckus, but Marci knew better. Smokey would understand that if they were out on the ledge, a hundred feet above the ground, things were not going well, and he should wait for directions.

Smokey stood for a moment contemplating what he could do to help, but for once, it seemed there was nothing for him to do. He investigated the base of the building to see if there was any way for him to get up to where the children were, but the only thing that could be even remotely useful were two large banners hanging from the northeast and southeast corners of the fourth-story ledge where the children were standing. The banners had been hanging there for months in commemoration of the Temple's upcoming one hundred tenth anniversary, and they were meant to be nothing more than an advertisement. But to Smokey's clever mind, they were much more than that.

He ran as fast as he could over to the southeast corner of the building and began to gnaw at the thick knot that fastened the banner to an iron hook at the base of the building.

"What's he doing?" Kay whispered.

"I think he's trying to get us down," Marci replied.

As soon as these words passed her lips, she heard a muffled voice from inside the Temple say, "Hey, is this window supposed to be unlocked?"

This was followed by a slow creaking from the window near the northeast corner of the building. Kay had the misfortune of being the one standing closest to that window, so it was she who had the closest view as it slowly opened and a hooded head poked out. The man turned to his right and his eyes locked with Kay's.

Kay turned, looked at the others, and began snapping her fingers at lightning speed. She was too afraid to speak, but the horrified look on her face and her frantic finger-snapping told Marci and Archie all they needed to know.

"Follow me," Marci whispered as she slid along the ledge to her right.

"Who are you?" yelled the hooded man, who was now leaning fully out the window, astonished to see three children out on the dangerous precipice.

"Move it!" Kay yelled, suddenly regaining her powers of speech.

"What are you kids doing out here?" The hooded man stuck his foot on the ledge and struggled to get the rest of his rotund frame through the window.

"Come on, guys, let's go!" Marci yelled over her shoulder.

Meanwhile, Smokey had untied the banner from the base of the building and was holding it tightly in his powerful jaws, slowly backing away from the building. It soon became obvious that Smokey had made a flimsy, but possibly workable, slide to get them off the ledge. Despite their amazement at Smokey's resourcefulness, none of them were particularly wild about sliding over a hundred feet down a thin, synthetic banner.

Or, as Kay put it to Marci, "Are you nuts? You don't really expect us to slide down that thing, do you?"

Marci reached the corner of the ledge, turned back over her shoulder, and yelled, "Yup, unless you want to get to know the guys in the hooded robes!"

With those words, Marci took a deep breath, scooted her

legs onto the banner, and pushed herself off the ledge and onto the makeshift slide.

She slid down the banner faster than she'd expected, and she had to shift her weight back and forth several times to make sure she didn't slip off. Overall, though, it was very similar to going down a water slide.

When Marci reached the bottom, she landed hard on the grass. She quickly crawled back to the banner, patted Smokey on the head, and grabbed hold of the left side of the banner while Smokey continued to hold the right side in his mouth.

"Come on guys, move it!" Marci yelled. The large Mason had made it out the window and was now awkwardly shuffling his way along the ledge toward Kay.

"Here goes nothin'," Archie said as he reached down to find the banner, swung his legs over the side, and slid down toward Marci and Smokey. Fortunately, his descent was much smoother than Marci's because the banner was sturdier with both Smokey and Marci holding on.

When Archie reached the bottom, he too grabbed hold of part of the banner to make the ride smoother for Kay, who flew down even faster than he had. When Kay reached the bottom, the others quickly released the banner and let it blow harmlessly in the wind so the Mason couldn't use it to slide down.

"Let's get out of here before they come after us!" Kay yelled. She put Marci on her back and led Archie around the side of the Temple and into the woods where they had left the bike and wheelchair.

In no time at all, the three were pedaling furiously through the trees and out into the light of the parking lot. Marci led the way, but as she began to head across the parking lot and out to King Street, she realized that might be a bad idea. King Street sloped down through the neighborhoods of Alexandria to the riverbank. If they turned left toward home, as she'd been planning, they'd be pedaling uphill the whole way, which would slow them down. Marci wondered whether it would make more sense to head in the other direction—until the Masons answered her question for her. Several of them suddenly ran out from the side entrance of the Temple, blocking the kids' way to King Street.

Marci spun her chair around on a dime.

"That way, that way, that way!" she yelled frantically, pointing toward the southern slope of Shooter's Hill. Kay and Archie quickly reversed course, but Smokey stopped to growl at the Masons, who were now racing to get into their cars and give chase.

"Come on, boy!" Marci yelled.

Smokey gave one more angry bark toward the Masons before he turned and followed the fleeing children.

As the kids left the parking lot and raced down the grassy slope, Marci realized they had chosen a much better escape route. The hill was steep enough that when they reached the bottom, it would spit them out onto the sidewalk along Duke Street with enormous momentum. Also, there was no way for the Masons to get down to Duke Street in their cars unless they decided to drive on the grass.

Unfortunately, as they began careening down the southern slope of Shooter's Hill, the children saw headlights bearing down on them. Clearly, the Masons had no qualms about driving their cars down the grassy hill.

As Marci looked back over her shoulder, she saw three distinct sets of headlights speeding after them. She knew there was no way they could outrun the cars for very long.

"Head for the train tracks!" she yelled.

Kay and Archie followed Marci's lead. When they reached the bottom of the hill, instead of turning on to the sidewalk and heading west, they sped directly across both lanes of Duke Street and shot down the rocky embankment that led to the train tracks on the other side. During daylight hours, they never would have been able to cross Duke Street without stopping to wait for traffic, but at this hour, with few cars on the road, it wasn't a problem.

As they bumped and thumped down the craggy hillside, neither Marci nor Kay could afford to take their eyes off the ground lest they make a wrong move and flip over. As a result, they had no way of knowing just how close behind the Masons were.

As it turned out, while the Masons had no problem driving their cars down the grass on Shooter's Hill, none of them had any desire to blow out all their tires following the children down to the train tracks. Instead, they pulled their cars over on the sidewalk alongside Duke Street and gave chase on foot.

"They're heading to the trains!" one of the Masons yelled.

When Marci looked back over her shoulder, she saw the Masons stumbling down the embankment with flashlights in their hands. She had never been in the rail yard before, but she had passed over it a number of times on the Metro. She knew that it came to an end at the tunnel that led to the Eisenhower Avenue station, and there was no way out of the rail yard except the way they had come. If the Masons were going to give chase, she wasn't sure how they were going to get away.

Marci's heart was racing as she tried to think of what they could do next. As she pedaled furiously between the boxcars sitting idly in the rail yard, it occurred to her that some of them might be empty. Apparently, the same thing had occurred to Kay, because at that moment she cried out, "Marci, we need to find a boxcar to hide in!"

"Good thinking!" she called back.

They continued pedaling. The situation looked bleak. None of the boxcar doors were open, and each was secured with a heavy padlock.

"Stop!" Kay cried out as she slammed on the breaks of the tandem bike. "This one doesn't have a lock!"

She ran over to the nearest boxcar and laboriously pulled the door to the sidecar open. She helped Archie into the boxcar after the two of them flung their bike inside. Kay lifted Marci into the boxcar and hoisted her wheelchair in before climbing in herself. Then Smokey leapt in, and the three kids all worked together to slide the heavy boxcar door shut.

"Kay, you're a genius!" Marci whispered.

"Well, let's not count our chickens before they've hatched," Archie replied. He could hear the Masons still giving chase.

The kids sat down on the steel floor of the boxcar and tried to be as quiet as possible. They each began to wonder the same thing: *What is that smell?*

"Did anyone happen to notice what was inside this boxcar?" Kay asked.

"No," Marci replied, "but it smells funny."

"Are we in a boxcar full of bananas?" Archie sniffed the air.

Kay had a tiny flashlight in her tool belt, so she pulled it out to examine their surroundings. Sure enough, they were indeed in a boxcar full of bananas.

"Yup, they're bananas," Kay whispered to her brother.

"Well, at least we won't starve to death in here," Marci said.

Kay shushed her. "It's the Masons," she whispered.

They could each hear their own hearts beating as they tried with all their might not to make the slightest noise.

"Where could they have gone?" one of the Masons yelled outside the boxcar, startling the children.

"Those kids better hope I don't get a hold of 'em," another man muttered directly outside the boxcar.

The kids' hearts almost stopped at the sound of those words. Kay gripped her hands tightly together to keep from snapping her fingers. Archie tried not to even breathe lest the men outside hear him. Even the usually unflappable Marci could feel the sweat of fear beading on her forehead. Each second felt like an eternity as they listened to the men walking around outside the boxcar.

Fortunately, after several minutes, the voices outside grew fainter until the children could no longer hear anything except their own breathing.

"I think we're in the clear," Archie whispered, finally able to relax a bit and breathe easily. "What do we do now?"

"I say we stay here for the night," Marci said.

"But what about our parents?" Kay asked.

"We have to get downtown to the American History Museum first thing tomorrow," Marci replied. "If we go home, there's no way we'll be able to get there tomorrow."

"Sure there is," Archie said. "We can just ask Sofia or Joseph to take us."

"No," Marci replied, "if we go home, we're going to spend all day tomorrow in Hector's hospital room. I'd rather spend tomorrow looking for something that could save his life than sitting around the hospital doing nothing."

"But we're going to get in so much trouble." Kay imagined how her parents would react if she and Archie weren't in their beds in the morning. "And Mom and Dad are going to be worried sick."

"Don't worry, Kay. I'll handle it," Archie replied. "I'll call them first thing in the morning and leave a message to let them know they don't need to worry about us."

"Trust me," Marci said, "our parents would be a lot more disappointed with us if they knew we gave up on something that could have saved Hector's life."

"Alright," Kay replied. "You convinced me."

"Thanks, guys," Marci said. "I'll need all the help I can get."

"Anything for Hector," Archie said.

"He'd do the same for us," Kay added.

None of them had thought much of Hector during the excitement of the last few hours. Now, as they laid down on the steel floor of the rail car and began to doze off, Hector was on all of their minds. He was the reason they had risked so much already, and he was the reason they would risk so much more in the days ahead.

9

A sliver of sunlight shone through the boxcar and pierced Marci's eyelids as she began to wake up. It usually took her a few minutes to rise in the morning, but this morning she sat right up because something was terribly wrong. Was it a hurricane? An earthquake? A tornado? She looked around in confusion until the smell of bananas filled her nostrils, and she remembered where she was. The rumbling she felt and the wind she heard rushing by was not that of a hurricane, an earthquake, or a tornado, but of a moving train.

Marci leaned over to Kay and shook her awake.

"Kay, the train's moving!"

"What?" Kay mumbled as she tried to roll over.

They had all fallen asleep close to five a.m., so it was no wonder that each of the children and Smokey had slept in despite rolling along in a train at about thirty miles per hour.

"Wake up!" Marci implored, shaking Kay again.

Kay slowly pulled herself up on her elbows and looked around. It was clear that she too had momentarily forgotten where she was.

"We're moving!" she exclaimed as she looked around. "Where are we going?"

"I don't know!" Marci pulled herself over to the door, then got on her knees and slid it open, suddenly bathing the boxcar in sunlight. The noise of the rumbling train reverberated throughout, louder now, making it impossible for Archie to keep sleeping. It was a typically sweltering August day in Northern Virginia, and the temperature was already approaching ninety degrees even though it was only about 9:00 a.m.

"Oh, thank goodness," Kay said as she joined Marci in the doorway. "We're still in Virginia."

Indeed, they were passing through Crystal City in South Arlington, about to cross the bridge over the Potomac River into Washington, DC.

"Yeah," Archie said as he awoke, "but where are we going?"

"I have no idea," Marci replied. "But no matter where we're going, this train's going to have to pass through DC to get there."

"But will the train *stop* in DC?" Kay asked.

"Good question," Marci said as the train reached the bridge and began to pass over the river.

"You guys need showers," Archie said, sniffing his sister and their friend.

"Yeah, and you smell like roses," Kay said with a smirk.

"These freight trains pass through L'Enfant Plaza, don't they?" Marci asked.

L'Enfant Plaza was an area in the city named for Pierre Charles L'Enfant, the French architect and engineer who was commissioned by President Washington in 1791 to draw up a plan for the ten-mile square area that would eventually become Washington, DC. L'Enfant Plaza was chock full of federal buildings and offices, in addition to a train depot through which every train heading north from Virginia must pass.

"Yeah, I think you're right," Kay said, trying to recollect what she had seen the last time she had ridden an Amtrak train to New York with her family.

"But that doesn't mean it'll *stop* in L'Enfant Plaza," Archie said. "If the train passes through L'Enfant Plaza at thirty miles per hour but doesn't stop until it gets to Baltimore or Philadelphia, then we're in a whole heap of trouble."

"I don't see why it would stop at L'Enfant Plaza," Kay said. "That's a passenger station, not a place for a freight train to drop off its cargo."

"That's okay, we don't need it to stop," Marci said. "We can just jump off."

Kay did not love that idea. "Jumping off a speeding train can't be our only option," she said.

The others pondered their alternatives for a moment, but none of them could think of anything. If the train did not stop at L'Enfant, they would indeed have to jump.

"Well, the good thing about jumping from this train is that we won't have to worry about Mom and Dad killing us for sneaking out last night," Archie said.

"Why?" Kay asked.

"Because we'll break every bone in our bodies if we jump," Archie replied. "They can't be angry at us if we're all in the hospital."

The others wanted to tell Archie not to be so melodramatic, but for all they knew, he was right. After all, it certainly couldn't be good for anyone's health to jump from a moving train.

"What about our bike and your chair?" Kay asked. "Do we throw them out too?"

"And Smokey," Archie said. "Someone's going to have to hold him."

As the train rumbled on, Marci caught a glimpse of the Capitol Dome and realized they had to be getting close to L'Enfant Plaza.

"Come on," Marci said, "grab your bike!"

Kay and Archie rushed over to their bike and helmets and hurriedly gathered them up. Marci meanwhile pulled herself over to her wheelchair and climbed in, wondering just how she was going to get herself and the chair off the train in one piece. Fortunately, the train began to slow as it approached L'Enfant Plaza because one of the commuter trains was sitting at the station on the tracks that ran parallel to the freight train line.

"Are we stopping?" Marci asked.

"It doesn't feel like it," Archie said.

"I think we're just slowing down a bit as we go through the station," Kay added, snapping her fingers anxiously.

"Well, should we do it?" Archie asked.

"This is crazy." Regardless, Kay took their tandem bike and threw it off the train. Then she lifted Marci out of her wheelchair, handed her to Archie, and tossed the wheelchair out too. Kay then took Marci back in her arms and said to her brother, "You're going to have to take Smokey."

He dutifully scooped up the dog, who he could feel at his ankles, and clutched him tight. "Just tell me when it's safe to jump," Archie said.

"We'll go together on the count of three," Kay said. "One, two, three!"

With a deep breath, Kay and Archie leapt off the train, falling briefly through the air before landing on the gravel that lined the train tracks. As they hit the ground, they were able to keep their footing despite the extra weight they were each carrying.

"That wasn't so bad!" Marci exclaimed.

"Easy for you to say," Kay replied with a smirk. She slung Marci around so she could latch onto her back.

"Let's go see if our bike and chair had it as easy as we did," Archie said, putting Smokey down. He then unfolded his white cane and tapped it on the gravel as he walked back toward where he knew their bike must have landed.

When they got to the bike and chair, they were grateful to find that their vehicles had survived with only some minor nicks and scratches.

"Woo-hoo!" Marci exclaimed. "I don't know what my parents would have done to me if I'd broken this thing."

At that moment, the last car of the freight train passed, and the children realized the commuter train had gone as well. They suddenly felt odd, as if they were being watched. This stood to reason, because they were indeed being watched by the crowd of adults standing on the platform who had just disembarked from their commuter train.

"Uh, it looks like we have an audience," Kay whispered.

No sooner had she said that than a uniformed ticket agent who was standing on the platform began yelling at them.

"What are you kids doing over there? Stay there! Don't cross the tracks!" the middle-aged man yelled as he made his way down to the end of the platform.

"Oh boy, we gotta get out of here," Marci said. "If that guy gets hold of us, we'll never make it to the museum."

"Which way should we go?" Archie asked.

The ticket attendant was approaching from the only visible exit, a walkway that led out to Seventh Street.

"This way." Kay put their bike in the middle of the tracks

facing away from the approaching attendant. "Can you pedal your chair over these tracks?"

"I guess we're about to find out." Marci engaged the lever for her hand pedals and hoped her off-road wheels would do as well on train tracks as they'd always done in the woods.

As they started pedaling, Archie could hear another freight train and a commuter train off in the distance, approaching almost parallel to one another on the tracks.

"Kay!" Archie yelled, Smokey running alongside him. "I don't know if this is such a great idea!"

"Trust me!" she yelled over her shoulder.

The ticket attendant had climbed down onto the tracks and was still yelling for them to come back, but he was fading in the distance as the children rolled off in the direction of the approaching trains.

"Come back!" the attendant yelled in vain. He stopped chasing them and bent over with his hands on his knees to catch his breath.

The children kept pedaling on, but none of them were quite sure what Kay had in mind as the approaching train horns grew louder.

"Kay, what are you doing?!" Archie yelled to his older sister.

"Getting us out of here!" she yelled back. She abruptly jumped the tracks and then immediately hit the brakes. The tandem bike skid to a stop at the top of an embankment that led to Sixth Street. Kay leapt off her bike and pulled Marci's chair over the tracks just a few moments before the oncoming train passed.

Marci hadn't noticed that there was a path down to Sixth Street, but the always observant Kay had noticed it while they were on the train. And now that the trains were passing, they would provide cover for the children to carefully make their way down the embankment before the attendant could give chase again.

L'Enfant Plaza was always so busy in the morning with commuters rushing to work and tourists trying to navigate the five Metro lines that converged there that no one even noticed three kids emerging from the train tracks. Once they made it down the embankment, the three children and Smokey headed north up Sixth Street. When they got to Independence Avenue, they hung a left with Kay leading the way. She had only been to the National Museum of American History once on a school field trip, but she could remember that the school bus had gone up Fourteenth Street as it entered the city, so she knew they had to make their way in that direction.

Sure enough, eight blocks later, they arrived at Fourteenth Street. Kay turned right and headed north. Rush hour traffic was at full flow, but the sidewalk was wide open as they passed through the National Mall with the Washington Monument to their left and the Capitol Building in the distance to their right. They continued riding up Fourteenth Street for another few blocks until they reached Madison Drive. There before them at the corner sat a massive, square building that took up an entire city block: the Smithsonian Museum of American History.

"There it is," Kay said.

"What do we do now?" Archie asked.

"I think we need to call our parents," Marci answered.

"Where are we going to find a phone?" Archie asked, as none of the children were allowed to have their own cell phones yet.

"I've heard of these things called payphones," Marci replied, "although I can't say I've ever used one."

"Yeah, I've heard of those too," Kay added. "Let's see if we can find one."

As they rode up to the museum, Marci said, "Look, there's a blue phone right over there by the entrance. I bet that's a payphone."

Kay and Archie chained their bike to a rack outside the entrance to the museum and made their way over to the phone with Marci.

Marci dug into one of the pockets of her wheelchair for change, withdrew two quarters, and dialed home. As the line on the other end rang, she began to feel queasy. What would the Judge say? After the first ring, Marci allowed herself to fantasize about the possibility that the Judge wouldn't answer at all. Maybe she would be able to leave a voicemail rather than actually speaking to her father. Unfortunately, the Judge must have been waiting by the phone, worried sick about his missing daughter, and he quickly answered after the first ring.

"Hello?" the Judge said.

Marci could hear the worry in her father's voice, which only made her more nervous. As she failed to respond, the sound of the Judge's voice only grew more frantic.

"Hello? Is anyone there?" he asked.

"It's me, Marci," she replied, her voice quavering.

"Oh, thank God," the Judge replied frantically. "Where are you? Are you okay? Are you with Kay and Archie?"

Marci was disarmed by how frightened the Judge sounded. "Yeah, all three of us are here, and we're okay."

"Where are you?" the Judge said loudly into the phone, his voice almost cracking.

"I can't tell you, Dad," Marci replied, "but we're doing something to save Hector. I can't explain now, but I promise you'll understand when we're done."

"What?" the Judge said, his voice quickly transforming from fear to anger. "Tell me where you are!"

"I can't, Dad, but we're going to save Hector, I promise. We'll be home soon. Love you."

With that, Marci hung up the phone before the Judge had an opportunity to reply. As the receiver clanked down, she felt a rush of relief. She knew the Judge was fuming, but for the moment, she was simply glad to be off the phone.

"How did it go?" Archie asked.

"He's worried," Marci replied. "And now he's angry that I hung up on him, but at least he knows we're alright."

"What did he say?" Kay asked.

"Not much," Marci answered. "He pretty much just kept asking where we are."

Archie was up next, and when he called home, his mother answered. He repeatedly assured his mother that they were alright, but as Marci had done with the Judge, Archie refused to tell her where they were. After less than a minute, he could no longer bear his mother's worried pleas to come home. Archie told his mother he loved her, and once he and Kay had promised to be careful, he hung up the phone. They all stood in awkward silence for a moment after Archie let the receiver click down.

Archie eventually broke the quiet by saying, "That was the worst phone call of my life." Marci and Kay couldn't see his eyes behind the dark sunglasses he wore, but they could tell from his voice that he was holding back tears.

"Sorry about that," Marci said. "If you want to call her back to tell her to come get you guys, I'd understand."

"No," Archie replied, still trying to hold back tears, "we're in this with you."

"Yeah," Kay added, "Mom and Dad will understand when we get the Spearhead and save Hector."

At that moment, the doors to the museum opened, and an old security guard stepped out into the morning light. He had on a rumpled uniform and a huge key ring, from which hung about three dozen keys. His once-black shoes had been worn to a dull gray, and the cap he wore was so faded it looked as though it may have been older than the museum itself.

As the old man propped the door open, he peered out from under his cap at the children. At first, they thought he was going to scold them for being on the museum's front steps before it opened, but when his lips slowly crept up into an oddly welcoming smile, they knew they had nothing to worry about.

"Jeez, I've worked here since this place opened in 1964, and this is the first time I've found youngsters waiting at the front door when I opened up in the morning."

"Sorry, sir. We're not trespassing, are we?" Marci asked.

"Goodness no," the man replied. "I wish I saw more youngsters waiting to get into this place in the middle of their summer vacation."

"Oh," Archie replied, "well, we just couldn't wait to get in."

"In that case, would you like the free tour?" the old man asked.

"Sure!" Archie replied.

"That's the spirit!" the old man said. "My name's Teddy. What are your names?"

Marci and Archie introduced themselves, but Kay clammed

up. Archie was accustomed to this, so he introduced his sister as she stared at the ground.

"Why can't she speak for herself?" Teddy asked. "And what's with the tool belt?"

"She's autistic," Archie said. "It can be hard for her to talk to people she doesn't know. And the tool belt is because she likes to build things. She's going to be an engineer when she grows up."

"Well, aren't you a regular group of misfits?" Teddy said. "A blind boy, a girl in a wheelchair, and a girl with autism."

Marci was annoyed and fired back, "We're not misfits, Mr. Teddy. We're *amazing*."

"Oh, I'm sorry, Marci," Teddy said, embarrassed. "I meant you're *amazing* misfits."

"That's more like it," Marci said, kind of liking the way "the Amazing Misfits" sounded.

"Now, what about that dog?" Teddy said.

The children looked at Smokey, and then at each other in bewilderment. In a flash, Archie thought of something.

"He's my service dog," Archie said. "Marci, can you hand me his leash?" He folded up his white cane and put it in his back pocket.

Marci took a leash out of the wheelchair pocket and handed it to Archie, who leaned down and hooked it onto Smokey's collar.

As they made their way into the museum, Teddy said, "You know, this is my favorite time of day in this old place. You can almost feel the nation's history come alive."

"Do you have any George Washington stuff?" Marci asked.

"Are you kiddin' me?" Teddy exclaimed. "We got tons of George Washington stuff. As a matter of fact, not too long ago, we got a treasure trove of Washington memorabilia on loan from the Masonic Temple in Alexandria. You kids ever been there?"

"Yeah," Archie replied with a smile, "we were there not too long ago."

"Great," Teddy said. "Well, why don't I show you our Washington exhibit?"

They soon found themselves heading down a wide hallway adorned with numerous artifacts from colonial times.

"That right there is the desk Thomas Jefferson used to write the Declaration of Independence," Teddy said, pointing to a small, mahogany lap desk. "And that's the disguise Sam Adams wore when he and the Sons of Liberty dressed up as Narragansett Indians during the Boston Tea Party."

"How did the museum get all this stuff?" Archie asked.

"Oh, some of it's been donated by families over the years, and some of it's on loan from other museums, like the stuff we got from the Masonic Temple," Teddy answered.

They walked past a couple other exhibits before they arrived at a large mural of George Washington on horseback in a driving snowstorm.

Teddy put his hand on Archie's shoulder and said, "And here it is, my boy. This is our new Valley Forge exhibit. We've got authentic pots and silverware from Valley Forge, an original musket—not to mention General Washington's very own field trunk, right there."

The children stared at the large wooden trunk, which had a camp stool beside it, along with a pewter plate, some silverware, and a silver cup resting on top. This was what they had come for, but none of them could quite believe they were now staring right at it.

As they surveyed the trunk, each of them tried to find some sign of the piece of the Spearhead. Unfortunately, if it was there, they couldn't see it.

They spent the rest of the morning walking around the museum, getting their private tour from Teddy. He delighted in telling them all kinds of stories about the various exhibits, while the children silently schemed out a plan for getting their hands on that field trunk. As they went through the museum, they also scoped out potential hiding places in case they needed them for when they returned to look for the Spearhead. They noticed lots of the exhibits had large curtains near them, which might come in handy later if they needed to hide.

They returned to the first floor of the museum after seeing every exhibit it had to offer. Teddy turned to the kids and said, "Well, that's all I've got. Thanks for letting me show you around the place."

"Thanks for having us, Teddy," Marci replied. "We couldn't have asked for a better tour guide."

"My pleasure," the old man said. "Things get a little slow around here during the summer while school's out. It warms my heart to see youngsters here on their own." Then Teddy cocked his head to one side, scratched his chin, and said, "Which makes me wonder, what are you kids doing here on your own? Aren't your folks around or something?"

Archie quickly stepped in with an explanation. He hated telling Teddy another fib, but he knew he had to do it or Teddy would end up calling their parents.

"Oh, our dad works just up the street," he said. "We're meeting him at his office for lunch."

"And look at the time," Marci said, checking her watch. "We should really get going. Thanks again for the tour, Teddy."

She held out her hand to shake Teddy's. "Let's go, guys."

"Thanks, Teddy," Archie said, shaking the man's hand as well.

"Yeah, thanks," Kay said quietly without extending her hand to shake.

"She speaks!" Teddy said. Kay had been totally silent for their tour.

Teddy's comment would have normally annoyed Kay, but he seemed like he meant well, so she giggled a little as she turned to leave.

"So, what now?" Archie asked once they were all outside.

"I wish we *were* going to lunch right now," Marci replied. "I'm pretty hungry."

"Could we get some lunch?" Kay asked. "We could all use some food."

"Okay," Archie said, "how much money do we have?"

Each of the children reached into their pockets and dug for the money they had extracted from their piggy banks the night before.

"Let's put all our money together and count it," Archie said.

The children all put their money in a pile on the sidewalk, and Kay began to count it.

"Fifty-one dollars and eighty-seven cents," she announced a moment later.

"We better find all the pieces of the Spearhead fast," Marci said. "That seems like a lot of money, but fifty bucks won't last us too long in the city."

"You're right. We have to be careful with that money," Kay said.

"Which means we've got to eat cheap," Archie added.

"Why don't we just go get a bunch of candy bars at a drug store? That won't cost much at all."

Kay shook her head.

"Candy bars won't fill us up," she said.

"Why don't we get some half-smokes over there?" Marci suggested, pointing to a hotdog vendor on the sidewalk.

"Good idea," Kay said as Archie too nodded his approval.

When they were done munching on their lunch of half-smokes, which they shared with Smokey by tearing off pieces, they had a lot of time to kill before the American History Museum closed, so they visited each of the museums on the mall. Archie's favorite was the Natural History Museum, while Marci's was the Air and Space Museum. Kay could easily have spent all day at the Museum of the American Indian.

As the shadow of the Washington Monument began to stretch toward them, Kay and Archie collapsed in a heap on the grass on the National Mall while Marci slumped in her chair.

"Whoa, we sure covered a lot today," Archie said from his spot in the grass.

"What time does the American History Museum close?" Marci asked.

"In thirty minutes," Kay said. "What's our plan for getting the first piece of the Spearhead?"

"I've been thinking about that," Marci said, "and a couple of us are going to have to go in there and stay after the museum closes."

"How are we going to do that?" Archie asked.

"Hide in one of the bathrooms," Marci said.

The others gave her a puzzled look.

"I saw it in a movie," she went on. "You hide in the stalls, put the seat down, and crouch on top of the toilet so your feet can't be seen under the stall. When the security guard looks under the stall for feet, it'll look like no one's there."

It seemed too simple, but Kay and Archie couldn't think of anything better.

"Alright, now we just need to figure out how to get out once we get the Spearhead," Kay said.

"Do you think an alarm will go off when we take the Spearhead?" Archie asked.

"Most likely," Marci said. "The whole place is probably covered in alarms. There's some expensive stuff in there."

"So what do we do when the police show up?" Archie asked. "We won't be much help to Hector if we're sitting in jail. And I bet when the police go in, the security system will lock down all the doors."

They all sat in silence for a few moments and pondered this question. As usual, Marci had an idea.

"I think I've got something that'll work," she said. "But listen up, 'cause we don't have much time before the museum closes."

Kay and Archie were sitting cross-legged on the toilet seats in the ladies' room on the second floor of the American History Museum. The museum had been closed for about two hours, and since then, they had been sitting there in complete silence, waiting for a security guard to check the bathrooms.

"Kay," whispered Archie.

"What?" she whispered back.

"I can't feel my butt anymore," he replied. "How much longer do we have to stay in here?"

"Until the guard comes by," she answered. "It shouldn't be too much longer."

"How do you know that?" Archie asked.

Kay, in fact, had no idea when the security guard would be checking the stalls. She was simply hoping that it would happen soon, because she too was beginning to wonder how much longer she could sit on the cold porcelain seat.

"I just know it," Kay replied. Then she added, "I hope Marci's doing alright outside."

Marci and Smokey were hiding outside near the entrance to the museum, waiting for the moment when they would spring into action.

"I bet Marci smartened up and went home," Archie said with a scowl.

Kay was about to scold him for his negative attitude when they finally heard the sound they had been waiting for: footsteps coming down the hall.

They drew their feet tighter to their bodies and tried to calm their breathing. They knew the only way to escape unnoticed was to remain utterly silent. If they were caught at this stage, their entire adventure would be over.

As the door creaked open, the children felt their hearts begin to pound almost as hard as they had out on the ledge of the Masonic Temple. They couldn't see the security guard who had just entered the restroom, but they could clearly hear their footsteps.

After a few more footsteps, they heard the unmistakable sound of the water running, followed by the sound of the guard tearing off some paper towel to wipe their hands, and then a few more footsteps. This was the moment of truth. At this point, they were either going to walk out of the bathroom or begin checking the stalls. One step, followed by another, followed by another—and then the sound they had been waiting for: the door to the bathroom opened, and half a second later it swung shut. Archie and Kay simultaneously let out huge sighs of relief. Now they just had to give the guard a few minutes to get farther down the hall before they could swing into action.

After just over a minute had passed, Archie exclaimed, "I can't take it anymore! My rear end is killing me."

With that, they both dismounted from their porcelain thrones and limped out of the stalls.

"Oh boy, that was the worst," Archie said as he hobbled around.

"Tell me about it," Kay said, rubbing her sore bottom.

Once they had recovered, Kay gingerly pushed the bathroom door open and poked her head out. She looked up the hall one way, then down the other. Seeing nothing but darkness, she exhaled deeply, pushed the door wide open, and grabbed Archie's hand so he could follow her out.

"Let's go check out Valley Forge," Kay whispered.

They made their way slowly down the hall, with Kay's head constantly on a swivel for any sign of security guards and Archie's ears pricked up for the slightest sound. Fortunately, there was nothing to be seen or heard. In under two minutes, they were down on the first floor, standing in front of the Valley Forge exhibit.

For the second time in less than twelve hours, the children found themselves standing before the heavy wooden field trunk that they believed held the first piece of the Spearhead that might save Hector. Unfortunately, at such a late hour, the lights were all out around the exhibit, and Kay could barely see a thing.

"It's really dark around this exhibit," Kay said. "I'm afraid to go any closer or I might knock something over."

"Don't worry," Archie said. "I had Marci describe the entire exhibit in detail to me earlier today."

With those words, he stepped over the velvet rope around the exhibit and navigated his way through the exhibit until he was standing over the field trunk. He then leaned over and carefully felt around in the open trunk for anything that felt close to what he thought might be the Spearhead. After a moment, he picked something up, and returned to where Kay was standing. Kay could see that the object Archie was holding looked like a jagged piece of glass—and it was not in the shape of a proper spearhead.

"What's that?" she asked.

"I'm pretty sure it's the piece of the Spearhead we've been looking for," Archie said. "Nothing else in that trunk felt like it could be made out of quartz."

Suddenly, bright yellow lights came on over the exhibit and deafening sirens began to blare. Kay gasped and clapped her hands over her ears with her eyes squeezed shut. Like many autistic people, she hated sudden or loud noises.

Archie reached out and found her elbow with his free hand. "That's our cue to get to our hiding place," Archie said in Kay's ear while tugging on her arm.

Kay clenched her teeth and led the way out of the exhibit. "I hope you grabbed the right thing."

The two of them moved as fast as they could to the Declaration of Independence exhibit. Beside it hung a large red velvet curtain that the two children could comfortably fit behind without being seen.

No sooner had they slipped behind the curtain than they heard the footsteps of the security guards rapidly descending onto the Valley Forge exhibit.

"What's missing?" one of the guards asked.

"I—I don't know," one of the other guards replied. "It doesn't look like anything's missing."

"Well, something's gone," said a third voice. "Those sensors only go off if the exhibit is touched. Someone took something. You two search the area. I'm gonna go check the surveillance video before the cops get here so we'll know who we're looking for."

"Yikes," Archie whispered, "we didn't think about the surveillance video."

"Nothing we could do about that," Kay whispered back.

"Are all the doors locked down?" one of the guards asked.

"Yup, no one can get out," the other guard replied. "Our thief is definitely still right here in the building."

Archie and Kay felt golf ball-sized lumps form in their throats. Kay gripped her hands tightly to try and keep herself from snapping her fingers. Archie could sense her anxiety, so he reached over and put his left hand on her hands to try and calm her.

OOO

Outside, Marci and Smokey hid in the bushes not far from the main entrance to the building. Their job was to keep an eye out for any police and find a way to keep the doors open if the police entered the museum. If they weren't able to keep a door open, then Archie and Kay would have no way of getting out of the building.

Both Smokey and Marci had occasionally fallen asleep at their post throughout the evening, but since the alarms inside the museum had started going off about five minutes earlier, they were both on pins and needles. Just as Marci was beginning to wonder what was taking the police so long, she saw flashing lights and heard the telltale sirens. She clutched Smokey's collar to make sure he didn't run toward the cars. Three police squad cars pulled up a moment later and screeched to a halt outside the museum. When the six police officers arrived at the back door, one of the museum security guards was there to meet them. He opened the door for the police and said, "Our thief is still in here—we just have to find him."

"Then let's do it," one of the officers said as they filed in through the door.

As the last officer disappeared through the door, Marci let

go of Smokey's collar and whispered, "Okay boy, go hold the door!" Smokey took off as fast as he could. The door swung slowly, giving Smokey more than enough time to wedge his body in before it could close. Moments later, Marci wheeled up and wedged a rock in the doorway, giving Archie and Kay a way to get out of the building safely. She and Smokey then retreated back to their hiding place and waited for Kay and Archie.

OOO

Kay and Archie were still sweating bullets as they stood behind the curtain and heard the footsteps of the guards around them. They wondered what would happen next, but neither of them had noticed that the curtain they were standing behind had actually been drawn across a large window that was about six feet wide and ten feet tall.

Nor had they noticed the shadowy figure who was standing right behind them on the ledge in front of the window.

"Hi kids," he whispered menacingly.

Kay and Archie almost screamed when they heard the man's voice. Kay looked over her shoulder to see who it belonged to. To her surprise, the man wasn't dressed like a police officer or a security guard, but a cat burglar.

"Don't say a word," said the man as his eyes locked on Kay's. "Just give me the Spearhead."

Archie said nothing as he held his hand out and grudgingly gave the man the object he was holding.

The man studied the jagged white object in his hand quizzically before whispering with a sneer, "This is it?"

Archie nodded. Kay could tell from the man's perplexed look that he had been expecting Archie to hand him the full

Spearhead. *This guy doesn't know the Spearhead is in three pieces,* Kay thought.

The man slipped the piece of the Spearhead into a small bag slung across his chest. Then, before turning to unlock the latch on the window, he said, "Nighty night, children."

As soon as the words escaped his lips, he pushed the window open and jumped out. They were still on the first floor, so it was only a three-foot drop from the window ledge to the grass below. The window was on the front of the building, so the burglar emerged from the museum no more than thirty feet from where Marci was hiding.

"Who's that?" Marci whispered aloud as the burglar slipped down from the window.

Smokey didn't know who he was, but he was certain the strange man was up to no good, so he sprang into action. In a matter of seconds, Smokey was bearing down on the man, who never even saw him coming.

Smokey grabbed on to a pant leg, and the man tripped, falling flat on his face and slamming into the ground. The strap across his chest snapped and sent his bag flying onto the sidewalk.

While the man lay on the ground groaning and wondering what had just happened, Smokey raced over and retrieved bag from the sidewalk, gripping it tightly in his teeth.

"Come here, boy," Marci called from behind the tree where she had been watching all the action. Smokey happily obeyed and ran into Marci's waiting arms.

At that moment, Archie and Kay climbed out of the window, and Marci waved them over.

"Did you see a scary lookin' guy jump out of that window?" Kay asked.

Marci nodded and pointed at the man, who was about thirty feet away from them as he pulled himself to his feet and looked at the children with menacing eyes.

"He's got the Spearhead," Kay said.

"Did he put it in that bag?" Marci asked, pointing at the bag that Smokey was still clutching in his jaws.

Kay didn't answer, but Marci could tell from the grin on her face that the Spearhead was in the bag.

"Okay guys, no time for chit-chat," Archie said. "Those security guards and police will be out here any minute. Let's get our bike!"

Kay pet Smokey on the head, grabbed the bag from his mouth, and then led the other children down the street as they raced off to their bike.

The burglar had gotten to his feet, but the police were now emerging from the museum and had set their eyes on him. He wanted to chase the children, but his only avenue of escape was to run in the opposite direction to where his car awaited. Ruefully taking one last look at the children escaping with his bag, the burglar turned and ran west down Constitution Avenue toward his car.

The police emerging from the museum didn't even notice the children and small dog, who were by now at the end of the block and turning the corner toward the bushes where the bike was hidden. But they did notice the burglar, clad in black and limping as he struggled to make his way down the street.

OOO

While the police gave chase, one law enforcement officer was not interested in the burglar. FBI Agent Steven Nighthawk had been watching from his unmarked car across the street on Constitution Avenue as the entire scene unfolded. When the children rode off in the darkness, he didn't radio any of the police officers. Instead, he followed slowly behind the children, careful to stay far enough back that they wouldn't notice. He watched silently as the children rode down beneath the Fourteenth Street Bridge and settled in to sleep like vagrants for the few hours of darkness that remained.

Normally, a child in a wheelchair, two more on a tandem bike, and a dog fleeing the scene of a robbery would have gotten more of a response from Agent Nighthawk, but not that night. For reasons only he understood, he was content to merely watch over the children as they huddled together under the bridge and drifted off to sleep.

11

At 7:00 a.m. on Capitol Hill, an unshaven, haggard-looking man strode up to the security gate outside the main entrance of the Senate side of the Capitol. He was clad all in black, just as he had been the prior evening during his failed burglary at the American History Museum.

The security guards were prepared to shoo him away, but he startled them by brandishing a security badge indicating that he was on the senate majority leader's staff. The man walked straight past them.

"Jeez, Senator Maxwell's standards have really slipped," one of the security guards said. He shook his head at the man who had limped past them and was now making his way toward the restricted elevator that led directly to the senate majority leader's office.

As the elevator rose and the doors opened, the man stepped out and winced in the bright, sunbathed vestibule of Senator Maxwell's palatial office.

"May I help you?" asked the prim, elderly woman behind the receptionist's desk.

He didn't even need to answer her question, as the senator

himself suddenly emerged from his office and called out, "Oh, good, the messenger's here. Come right in, young man."

The man in black limped past the smiling senator, who winked at his secretary. She knew this mysterious man was no messenger. The senator then turned on his heels and quickly closed his office door behind him.

"So, where is it?" he said excitedly.

The man in black was slumped on the couch in the middle of the senator's office. "Don't got it," he mumbled.

"What do you mean by 'don't got it'?" the senator asked, his voice markedly less pleasant than it had been a moment before.

"It means what it means," the man grumbled. "It means I don't got it."

"But I don't understand," the senator snapped. "The news is all over the papers and the morning shows about the burglary at the American History Museum last night. Everyone's perplexed because the burglar took only a stone of some sort from the Washington exhibit."

"Yeah, that sounds about right," the man in black replied.

"So where is it?" the senator repeated, raising his voice.

"Some kids got it," the man in black mumbled.

"Kids?" the senator asked suspiciously. "How many of them were there?"

"Don't know," the man replied. "Two or three, maybe. They had a dog with them. That's how they tripped me up and got the stone. I had the thing right in my hands, and they took it."

"What are you talking about?" asked the senator, pensively pacing the room.

The man in black explained what had happened, describing how he had been making his escape when he was tripped up by a dog. He said the children had headed one way down Constitution Avenue, while he'd had to go in the opposite direction to evade the police.

"So you have no idea where they are now?"

"Nope," the man replied. Against his better judgment, he began to nod off, exhausted as he was from staying up all night making sure the police weren't following him. The senator's couch was very plush, and the man in black would have liked to fall asleep right then and there.

"Go find them!" The senator unfurled a wad of cash from his jacket pocket.

"Come on, man, I haven't slept since yesterday," the man in black replied.

"I'll double what I'm paying you," the senator said. He unpeeled several large bills and held them out to the tired man.

"How am I s'posed to find 'em?" the man asked.

"That's your problem," the senator replied. "But I need you to find them right away."

"That reminds me," the man said, "this wasn't no spearhead. It was more like a rock or something."

"What?" the senator replied. "Are you sure they grabbed the right thing?"

"Yeah, I'm pretty sure," the man replied. "There wasn't anything else in there that looked like it could be a piece of a spearhead."

"Hmm, strange," the senator said as he continued pacing the room. "Perhaps the Spearhead isn't in one piece. If so, that means they have to find at least one more piece before they'll have the whole thing." He turned to the man in black. "You may just have a second chance to get this right. I want you to go find those children and make sure you're watching them the next time they find a stone similar to the one you *almost* stole last night."

"I can't," the man grumbled. "I'm too tired."

"If you find them, I'll triple your fee," the senator said. Money was no object to him because he believed that he would be able to make a fortune selling the Spearhead to a drug company that would be interested in harnessing its healing powers.

"Alright," the man in black replied, "I'll see what I can do."

"I expect you'll do better than you did last night." The senator turned away from the man and glared out his window.

The man in black groused something in response and slowly made his way out the door.

As the man left, the senator continued to look out over Washington. People were just beginning to make their way to work as another day began in the Nation's Capital.

"I know you're out there," the senator hissed, "and I'm going to find you."

As the sun rose over the Potomac, the three children were slowly waking from their slumber beneath the Fourteenth Street Bridge. Marci rubbed her bleary eyes and looked around. The sun's reflection on the river was beautiful, and it gave her hope they would find the rest of the Spearhead and save Hector. As she began to stir, so did Kay and Archie.

"So, what's on the agenda for today?" Archie asked as he yawned.

"I'm pretty hungry," Kay groaned as she took some electrical tape from her tool belt to fix the broken strap on the sling bag that carried the piece of the Spearhead.

"I guess we should get something to eat first," Archie said. "How much money do we have left?"

"Just under forty bucks," Marci replied. "We've got enough left for three, maybe four meals, if we spend it wisely."

"Where can we get breakfast in the city?" Archie asked.

"There's a coffee shop on every corner," Kay replied. "I'm sure we can find bagels or something in one of them."

There was indeed a coffee shop on every corner, and the children rode to the nearest one, where they enjoyed a sparse breakfast of orange juice and bagels. They decided it would be too expensive for each of them to get cream cheese or butter on their bagels, so they ate them plain. As they ate breakfast, none of them noticed the black Grand Marquis parked across the street. It was the same car that had been parked adjacent to the overpass all night, the same car from which Agent Nighthawk had watched them. He was still watching.

"So, what's next?" Archie tore off a piece of his bagel and handed it to Smokey under the table. Each of the children gave Smokey some of their bagels, so by the end of the meal, Smokey had eaten more than any of them.

"Well," Marci replied, "I don't really know. What was the second part of that riddle we discovered in the Temple?"

Kay pulled her notebook from her pocket and turned to the page where she had transcribed the riddle.

"'He who searches for the Patawomeck head of the spear need not look far, for the first piece is near. It rests among those relics that traveled with the great man when liberty stood in the valley and darkness was at hand. When the first piece is found, there is still yet another, but to find it, one must go where the Patawomeck lie next to their brothers. If the so-journer finds them, the Spirit must be heard, for none other than she can reveal the third.'"

"Okay," Archie replied, "so the important part is: 'When the first piece is found, there is still yet another, but to find it, one must go where the Patawomeck lie next to their brothers.' What could that mean?"

"'Where the Patawomeck lie next to their brothers,'" Kay repeated to herself in a whisper. "'Where the Patawomeck lie next to their brothers'... What does it mean?"

"Who are the Patawomecks' brothers?" Marci asked. "Was there another tribe they were close to?"

"Back then, we were part of the part of the Powhatan Federation," Archie said, "along with about thirty other Algonquian tribes in Virginia, so that doesn't really narrow it down much."

"It's a burial ground," Kay said with a grin as the thought came to her. "I'd bet my life it's a Patawomeck burial ground."

"You mean the next part of the Spearhead is in a cemetery?" Archie said, his voice dripping with dread at the thought of hanging out in a cemetery searching for some old relic.

"I don't know," Kay said. "I don't think there are any Patawomeck burial grounds around here that anyone knows about. It's probably been built over, and no one even knows it's there."

"Yeah," Marci added, "it could be a school or a church or something, and no one would even know that underneath is an ancient Patawomeck cemetery."

"Okay," Archie said, "so if no one knows it's there, how are we supposed to find it?"

"That's the million-dollar question," Marci said. "How do you find an ancient burial ground that no one knows about?"

For several silent minutes, no one had any answers. Finally, the answer came to Kay.

"The Museum of the American Indian," Kay said. "If there's any information about old Virginia tribes and burial grounds, we'll find it there."

After finishing up breakfast, Kay and Archie hopped on their bike, and Marci engaged the hand pedals on her wheelchair. Then they all rode furiously down Independence Avenue toward the museum, which sat right on the National Mall between Third and Fourth Streets. The National

Museum of the American Indian was one of the newest buildings in the Smithsonian Institute, having opened in 2004. It was a five-story building near the Capitol that differed greatly in its appearance from other museums and government buildings in Washington, DC, most of which looked like rectangular Greek temples with white limestone pillars all the way around. In contrast, the National Museum of the American Indian building was curved all the way around and covered in beige Kasota stone so it resembled a mountain outcrop that had been carved out of the land by wind and water like one might find in the American West.

Kay and Archie locked up their bike on the rack outside the museum, and Archie put on Smokey's collar so he could pose again as his service dog. As they entered the building and stood in the lobby on the first floor, it occurred to the children that none of them knew where they were going or what they were doing.

"Uh, what are we going to do?" Archie asked.

"I don't know," Marci said. "Why don't we just ask if they have an expert on local tribes who we could talk to?"

They walked over to the information desk, where an elderly woman with a ball of gray hair atop her head sat squinting at a ledger through large Coke-bottle eyeglasses. She looked up from her paperwork and peered at the children with her large eyes.

"May I help you?" she asked with a sweet smile.

"Uh, yes," Marci said. "We were wondering if there's anyone here who we could talk to who's an expert on tribes local to the DC area."

"Let me think, let me think," she said, pensively tapping her lips with her index finger. "Of course! I think I know just the person who can help you." She wobbled around from behind her desk.

"Follow me, children," she said.

The kids did as they were told and followed the old woman as she walked out into the hallway, turned left, and shuffled a few feet to the elevator. As she hit the down button, she turned to them and apologized.

"The stairs would be faster, but these old hips of mine prefer the elevator," she said. "The man who can help you has his office down in the basement."

Marci, Kay, and Archie followed her into the elevator quietly. When they came to a stop at the basement and the elevator's bell dinged, the woman beckoned them out into the hall.

"Just down here to our right." She led them down a narrow hallway that was lined with offices.

"Mr. Axelrod is right down this way," she said. "He's our foremost expert on all the local tribes."

She rapped lightly on the last door at the end of the hallway.

"Come in," came a soft voice from the other side.

The old woman opened the door and stood aside so the man inside could see the children standing in the hallway.

"Mr. Axelrod," she said. "I'm sorry to disturb you, but I have some patrons here who are interested in discussing local tribes."

"Oh, my," the old man said, peering joyfully out from beneath bushy, salt-and-pepper eyebrows and a mane of wild gray hair. "Let them right in."

The woman smiled as she stepped out of the doorway and let the children into the small office, which could barely fit all of them.

"Just let me know if you need anything else, children." She started wobbling back to the elevator.

"So, you're interested in the local tribes, are you?" Mr. Axelrod said, jabbing a finger in the air.

"Yes sir," Marci replied.

"Well, you've come to the right place," the little bundle of gray-haired energy said. "I'm descended from the Anacostan Tribe that used to live right here in DC, and I teach a history class about all the local tribes at Howard University. Tell me, what exactly would you like to know about?"

"The Patawomeck," Archie said. "My sister and I are members of the Tribe."

"Ah, the Patawomeck!" Mr. Axelrod exclaimed. "I'm very familiar with your tribe. Let me start at the beginning, when the first humans crossed the land bridge from Asia into present-day North America . . . ."

"Actually," Marci broke in, "we're most interested in Patawomeck burial grounds."

"Burial grounds?" Mr. Axelrod asked.

"Yes, Patawomeck burial grounds," Marci said.

"Oh my," Mr. Axelrod said as he slumped back in his chair and rubbed his hands through his wild mass of hair. "Patawomeck burial grounds," he repeated. "That's a tricky one. As you know, the Patawomeck lived in Virginia along the river that bears their name, and there really aren't any known burial grounds in this area. Most of them were built over by colonizers."

"So, you can't help us?" Archie asked.

Mr. Axelrod furrowed his brow and crossed his arms as he searched his mind for some bit of information that might help, but he found none.

"I'm sorry children," he said, "but you've done the impossible: you've completely stumped me. I'm at a total loss. I'm very sorry."

"It's alright," Marci said. "Thanks anyway for your time."

As the children turned to leave, they were startled, Kay in particular, by the screech of Mr. Axelrod's chair against the floor. They turned to see him pushing his little body quickly out from behind his desk and rushing toward them.

"I might just have an idea," he muttered. He hurried past them through the door and turned left down the hallway. "Follow me to the map room," he said, beckoning. "I've got an idea for how we might be able to find what you're looking for. It's a long shot, but it just might work!"

The children rushed after the funny little man as he entered a large room at the end of the hall. The sign over the door read "Geography and Map Reading Room."

The room was massive, about the size of a full-length basketball court, and lined with row upon row of shelves, each bearing thousands of rolled-up scrolls.

Mr. Axelrod shuffled down one of the long aisles. When they had gotten about halfway down the long aisle, he grabbed the rolling library ladder and positioned it under a bookshelf labeled "Maps of Northern Virginia."

"Here we are," he said as he climbed the steps of the ladder. He stopped about halfway up the ladder and began unrolling some of the scrolls on the shelf before him. As the name of the room indicated, they were all maps.

As he perused the maps, the children stood in silence at the base of the ladder and waited.

Mr. Axelrod eventually lumped a dozen maps under his arm and climbed down the ladder. He unfurled them one after the other and spent about thirty minutes examining maps of Northern Virginia from the eighteenth and nineteenth centuries. He didn't say a word during all this time, and, mindful not to disturb him, the children didn't make a sound either. While they were grateful for his help, as the thirty-minute mark came and went, they began to wonder if they weren't wasting their time.

Then, all of a sudden, Mr. Axelrod broke the silence with a most surprising sound.

"Whoopee!"

Kay and Marci looked at one another, and Archie made a face as if he had just heard an alien landing from Mars.

"Whoopee! Whoopee! Whoopee!" Mr. Axelrod kept exclaiming as he held one of the maps aloft. "Follow me, children. I think I've hit pay dirt!" The large map was titled "Virginia Tribal Lands, 1805."

They eagerly followed him back up the aisle to the front of the room, where they all gathered around a table near the doorway. Mr. Axelrod placed the map in the center of the table and allowed the kids to look at it for a moment without saying a word.

"What should we be looking for?" Marci asked.

"That's a good question," Mr. Axelrod replied. "I can't say I've ever looked for a burial ground on a map before."

"What would a Patawomeck burial ground look like in real life?" Marci asked. "Did they have headstones and stuff?"

"No," Mr. Axelrod replied. "Local tribes didn't use headstones. They buried the dead collectively over time and built layers of dirt on top of each other. A Patawomeck burial ground would have been distinctive for its appearance as a single mound of dirt or a series of closely constructed mounds."

"What's that?" Marci asked, pointing at a spot on the map at the west end of Alexandria.

"That's a forest," Mr. Axelrod said.

"Oh," Marci replied glumly.

"Wait, young lady," Mr. Axelrod said as he bent down over the map so his nose was almost pressed up against it. "Do you see that lettering? I can't quite make it out."

Marci went in for a closer look and said, "It looks like it says, 'Potomac,' but it's faded, so I don't really know."

"Did you say 'Potomac'?" asked Mr. Axelrod.

"Yup," Marci replied. "But that doesn't make much sense—the river's a few miles east of there."

Mr. Axelrod stood up, put his hands on his hips, and unfurled a wide a grin across his small face. He then looked down at Marci and said, "Young lady, I think you just found a Patawomeck burial ground."

"What do you mean?" Marci asked. "It looks like it's supposed to be a forest."

She was correct. The area on the map they had been examining was marked with a series of upside-down Vs that indicated trees.

"I agree with you," Mr. Axelrod replied, "but as you must know, 'Potomac' was how the English spelled 'Patawomeck.' It's possible that this is just a marker for one of the last Patawomeck tribal areas, but that would surprise me, since the colonizers had driven the native people well outside of Alexandria by 1805. It may very well be a depiction of a set of ancient Patawomeck burial mounds."

"Where is that today?" Marci asked.

"Well, there's the old Alexandria-Leesburg Turnpike, which is present-day Route 7." Mr. Axelrod pointed to a road slightly to the north of the burial ground. "And there's Mountain Road, which later came to be known as Braddock Road." He pointed to a roadway that ran along the southern end of the burial ground. "Do you children know what stands on that land now?"

"It's hard to say without any landmarks," Marci replied. "Episcopal High School, Alexandria Hospital, and Fort Ward are the main landmarks in the west end of the city, but it doesn't look like any of them had been built yet."

"That's where Fort Ward is," Kay exclaimed, jabbing her finger at the spot on the map.

"Fort Ward is built on a Patawomeck burial ground?" Archie asked.

"It certainly looks that way," Mr. Axelrod said with a bemused smile. He was a little shocked that he and these curious children had just uncovered a bit of history that had been lost for over two hundred years.

"Thanks for all your help, Mr. Axelrod," Marci said. "We would have been chasing our tails without you."

"Oh, my pleasure young lady," he replied, still grinning at their discovery. "And thank you for coming here today. We just discovered something truly historic together. I can't wait to tell the media."

"Would you mind waiting a few days to tell the press?" Archie said. "Just so we can tell our mom and let her inform the rest of our tribe. I think it's important that a member of the Patawomeck Tribe tell them about this."

"Of course," Mr. Axelrod said. "I understand completely. It's been lost to history for the last two hundred years, so no harm keeping it to myself for a few more days. Thank you for coming by today. This is more excitement than I'm used to around here."

The children each thanked Mr. Axelrod, even Kay, and then

made their way down the hall to the elevator. Mr. Axelrod saw them off, then hurried back to his office after the elevator doors closed. He picked up the phone and quickly dialed.

"Hello, sir, it's Phillip Axelrod. Given your interest in the Patawomeck, I thought you might be interested to know that I just had some visitors. Yes, they were children, three of them and a dog. They were here asking about ancient Patawomeck burial grounds, and they're headed to Fort Ward in Alexandria right now. Yes sir, they just left."

After leaving the museum, the children debated how best to travel back to Alexandria. After some discussion, they decided the best thing to do was to spend some of their remaining money on a Metro ride to the Pentagon. From there, they could catch a bus to Braddock Road and stow their bike on the rack on the front of the bus.

Around two o'clock in the afternoon, they arrived at the bus stop at the corner of Howard Street and Braddock Road, directly across from Fort Ward.

Fort Ward was built in 1861 as one of the 161 earthwork forts that made up the defenses of Washington during the Civil War. It was named for Commander James H. Ward, the first Union naval officer to die in the Civil War. The fort never came under attack during the war and was abandoned soon after. Over the course of the next century, the fort fell into disrepair until the City of Alexandria restored it nearly a hundred years later as part of a Civil War preservation effort.

The children had been to Fort Ward dozens of times with their parents and their classes on field trips, so they were all familiar with its history. But as they stared across Braddock Road at the fort, for the first time, they saw something other than an old civil war fort—they also saw a cemetery.

As they crossed the street and rode on to the fort's grounds, it occurred to Marci that they were less than a mile down the street from the hospital where Hector lay, and where her parents were no doubt worried sick about her.

"I need to call the hospital and let the Judge and Mom know we're alright," she said.

"Yeah, we need to call our folks too," Kay said.

"Maybe we should look around a bit first, and then we can call them," Archie suggested. "You never know, maybe we'll find the rest of the Spearhead, and then we can talk to them in person when we take it down to the hospital."

"Well, what are we looking for?" Marci said. "I mean, we don't have much to go on except for that silly riddle that told us to go 'where the Patawomeck lie next to their brothers.'"

"I wish I knew," Kay said. "Let's snoop around for a while and see if we can find something that might give us some clues about what we're supposed to be looking for."

OOO

Marci and Kay spent their time searching in the woods and under bushes around the fort, while Archie used his cane to search the fort's open fields for any sign of earthen mounds that might indicate a burial ground. Unfortunately, after two hours of searching every inch of the old fort, they'd found nothing helpful. As they stood by the fort's main gate, they all looked glum, including Smokey. After a few depressing moments of silence, Archie tried to cheer everyone up.

"Why don't we go to Atlantis?" he suggested, referring to their favorite family restaurant at Bradlee Shopping Center, which was just down Braddock Road. "We just need to refuel, and then we'll be able to continue our search!"

"Do we have enough money for that?" Marci asked.

"No," Kay said. "We only have twenty-two dollars and seventeen cents left."

"Jeez," Archie replied, "that's not much. Maybe we should go to the supermarket and buy stuff for sandwiches."

"That's a good idea," Kay replied.

With their dinner plans decided, but their spirits still down, they slowly rode about a mile down the road toward the supermarket that sat next to Bradlee Shopping Center. At the supermarket, they purchased a loaf of bread, some bologna, a packet of cheese slices, and some bottled water. They pedaled back up the street to the softball field on the campus of Minnie Howard Junior High and ate their dinner on the bench in the dugout.

"We'll have to eat this for breakfast tomorrow too," Kay said as she munched on her sandwich.

"How much money do we have left now?" Archie asked.

"Not much," she replied, "only a little less than nine bucks. We might have to save this bologna in my backpack and eat it for dinner tomorrow night too."

"Gross," Marci said.

"Well," Archie piped in, "that just means we have to complete our mission before dinner tomorrow night."

When they were done eating, they rode their bikes back to Bradlee Shopping Center and found a payphone. They knew they had to call their parents, but none of them wanted to. Marci took the change from Kay's hand and bit the bullet.

"Here goes nothing." She inserted the money and dialed the number for the hospital.

"Yes, Hector Gonzales' room, please," she said. After a moment, she heard the Judge's voice on the other end.

"This is Judge Gonzales," he said.

Marci was startled by how tired and weary the Judge's voice sounded. If there was one thing that always struck people about the Judge, it was his deep baritone voice. For the first time, Marci thought his voice sounded quiet, almost weak.

"It's me," Marci said. "We just wanted to call to let you know we're alright."

There was a pause on the other end before the Judge replied, "Have you found what you were looking for?"

"Not yet," Marci said, "but we're not done looking."

Marci thought she heard a sniffle on the other end. She had never seen or heard the Judge cry before.

"Well, you keep lookin'," the Judge said. "You keep lookin'. How are the others?"

Marci almost fell over. The Judge wasn't angry. In fact, he wanted them to continue their quest. Marci could hardly believe what she was hearing, but rather than encouraging her, the Judge's words sent a chill down her spine. If the Judge wanted her to continue searching for something to save Hector, it meant his condition was truly desperate.

"Oh, they're good. Everyone's safe," she replied. "I think we're making real progress," she added, not believing it for a moment, but not wanting to dash the Judge's hopes.

Marci almost dropped the phone as she felt someone violently shaking her shoulder.

"What!?" she exclaimed as she turned around.

"Mrs. Kennedy." Kay pointed down the sidewalk.

Indeed, walking toward them down the sidewalk in the middle of the strip mall was Archie's and Marci's teacher from the previous year, Mrs. Kennedy. She would likely have heard by now that the children had been missing for the last two days, and she would call the police immediately upon spotting them. They had to leave, and in a hurry.

"I have to go. Kiss Hector for us." Marci dropped the receiver and hurried off with Kay and Archie before Mrs. Kennedy could get any closer. The children and Smokey tore off around the corner and hurriedly made their way back to Fort Ward.

"Goodbye, sweetie," the Judge said sadly on the other end, but no one was around to hear it.

Fort Ward closed every night at sundown, which meant in late August it closed at about eight o'clock. The children had been kicked out of the park's playground numerous times at the end of a day; they knew that the park ranger merely drove once around the park to make sure the place was empty before he left for the night. There was a gate at the front entrance that he would lock, but that could only keep cars out. Given the open nature of the park, there was really no way to keep people from entering after nightfall.

So, when night came, the children lay down in one of the rifle trenches that encircled the fort and put the bike and wheelchair down on the ground next to them. Once they heard the park ranger's truck drive by, they knew the park was theirs for the evening.

"Okay guys," Marci said, "let's head back out there and keep looking. If there's anything here, we're gonna find it."

Kay and Archie feigned smiles as they trudged off beside Marci to resume their search. But no one—including Marci—was optimistic that their second effort would be any more successful than their first. Sadly, by eleven o'clock they still hadn't found anything.

"Maybe we should get some sleep," Archie said. "We can start looking again in the morning."

The children were getting so disheartened that none of them really believed they would have the will to continue looking in the morning. However, none of them wanted to admit defeat just yet.

"Yeah," Marci said, "that sounds good."

With that, each of them, including Smokey, curled up on the grass next to the cannons and prepared to sleep. Despite all their frustration and disappointment, the children were so tired that they were all able to fall asleep in a matter of minutes.

OOO

Marci woke up in a fog—literally. She was exhausted, and as her heavy eyelids slowly opened, she thought for certain she was dreaming. She looked around and could scarcely see more than two feet in front of her face. A heavy fog had descended over the ground near the cannons where they had fallen asleep.

She lay motionless for a moment, trying to determine where this dream would take her, but as the seconds ticked away, she slowly came to realize she wasn't dreaming. The fog in the air was too real, and the smell of the grass beneath her cheeks was too authentic for this to be any kind of dream. *But if this isn't a dream*, she thought, *then who on Earth is playing that harmonica?*

Marci shot up and looked around to see where the strange sound was coming from. To her frustration, she could see very little through the blanket of mist that had descended over Fort Ward. One thing she could see was the moon above, which hung high in the pitch black sky and shone as brightly as ever. The moon indicated that not much time had passed since

Marci had fallen asleep a little after eleven o'clock. It gave her little comfort to know that she was in a fog-shrouded park, late at night, with some stranger lurking nearby playing the harmonica.

"Do you hear that?" someone whispered.

Marci nearly jumped out of her skin at the sound of those words, until she looked over and saw the speaker was only Kay. Unfortunately, her comfort was short-lived; she could tell from the alarmed look on Kay's face that she too had no idea where the harmonica was coming from.

"Yeah, I hear it," Marci replied. "But I don't know where it's coming from."

"Please tell me I'm dreaming," said Archie.

"I wish we were all dreaming," Kay replied, her voice a barely audible hush.

They all sat in silence, hoping the sound would go away. To their dismay, the tune of the harmonica only got louder as the unknown musician continued to play their oddly jubilant song.

"What song is that?" Marci asked.

Archie scrunched up his nose and thought for a moment before answering.

"It's 'Dixie,'" he said confidently.

"What?" Marci asked.

"You know," Archie whispered. "It goes, 'I wish I was in Dixie, hooray, hooray. In Dixie's Land, I'll take my stand, to live and die in Dixie.'"

"Oh," Kay replied, recognizing the familiar lyrics. "How do you know that?"

"I did a report for music class on songs from the Civil War. 'Dixie' is the most famous Confederate song from the war."

With all the whispering going on, it was only a matter of

time before Smokey woke up. When he did, he immediately began barking in the direction of the harmonica. The children winced. Smokey was usually so good at keeping quiet when they needed him to, but the high-pitched wailing of the harmonica was too much for even the most disciplined dog.

Marci reached over and cupped her hands around Smokey's mouth, muzzling him as best she could, but the damage had already been done. The moment Smokey's barking started, the harmonica stopped.

The children sat in petrified silence, waiting to see if the mysterious musician would come looking for the barking dog. A few tense moments passed before the children heard a sound that suddenly seemed much more welcoming than it had just a few minutes before: the sound of "Dixie" being played again.

The children sighed in relief.

"Well," Marci said after a few moments passed, "anyone want to come with me and see if we can find who that is?"

"Not really," Kay said.

"Yeah, are you crazy?" Archie asked.

"Maybe, but I'd rather not wait here and be scared all night," Marci said.

"Well, since my eyes aren't much help, I can take Smokey from you while you go check things out," Archie said.

"I'll go with you," Kay said reluctantly.

"Thanks." Marci handed Smokey off to Archie and crawled over beside Kay.

"Ready?" said Marci.

"No, but let's get it over with," Kay said.

With that, they both crawled away from the cannons and gingerly made their way across the pebbles that covered the ground between the cannons and the powder magazine in the Northwest Bastion of the fort. The harmonica sounded like it was coming from the open field just beyond the trench near the powder magazine. Marci hoped they would be able to sit atop the large wooden doors that covered the powder magazine and get a glimpse of the field. If they couldn't get a decent view from the powder magazine, they were going to have to crawl up to the other side of the trench and peer through the bushes that separated the trench from the open field.

After they made the slow, laborious crawl across the pearl-sized pebbles—being careful all the while not to make too much noise—they finally arrived at the wide white doors that covered the subterranean powder magazine.

Kay and Marci carefully crawled onto the doors and sat up very slowly. Then, moving carefully, Kay got to her feet.

"Can you see anything?" Marci asked.

"Nope," Kay replied. "I'm not tall enough. Why don't you get on my shoulders and see if you can get a better look?"

"Good idea," Marci replied eagerly.

Kay hoisted Marci onto her back and leaned over while Marci pulled herself onto Kay's shoulders. Kay could feel the sweat forming on her brow as she struggled to help Marci up without making too much noise. Once Marci had climbed up on Kay's shoulders, she peered through the fog to try and get a look at the field. The fog wasn't so bad on the other side of the hedge, but Marci was having trouble believing what she was seeing. She squinted to make sure her eyes weren't playing tricks on her.

"Can you see anything?" Kay whispered.

"Yup," Marci replied, her mouth ajar.

"Well, what do you see?"

"You won't believe me," Marci whispered. "I see a couple of Native Americans sitting around a campfire with some guys dressed up like Civil War soldiers."

"Marci, I'm serious," Kay responded testily. "Tell me what you see. This is no time for jokes."

"I'm not joking," Marci whispered. "I'm looking at two Native Americans and a few soldiers."

"I don't believe you," Kay said as she lowered Marci from her shoulders. "Come on." She motioned for Marci to follow her, then slowly crawled into the rifle trench and made her way up to the hedgerow. Kay crawled under the hedge, and as she peered through the fog, she couldn't believe her eyes. Just as Marci had described, there on the lawn seated around a campfire were two men dressed as old-timey Native American warriors, three men dressed as Union soldiers from the Civil War, and two others dressed as Confederate soldiers. Kay rubbed her eyes to make sure she wasn't hallucinating.

"See, I told you," Marci said with a smug little smile as she pulled herself up beside Kay.

Kay's jaw hung wide open until she said, "This is the weirdest thing I've ever seen."

As Kay and Marci lay on the ground watching the surreal scene around the campfire, Archie climbed up out of the trench and joined them under the hedge. His arrival barely startled Marci and Kay, who were still transfixed on the peculiar scene before them. Archie was still muzzling Smokey, who was growing increasingly restless.

"What's going on?" Archie hissed.

Kay began to describe the odd scene for him, but at that moment, the harmonica stopped again, and the strange men sitting around the campfire turned and looked in the direction of the hedge.

"You children can come out," said one of the Native Americans. "You've got nothing to fear."

None of the children moved or even breathed.

A few moments passed before one of the Confederate soldiers spoke. "Y'all ain't gonna get any gumbo if you stay under them bushes." He stirred the contents of a pot hanging over the campfire.

"They're talking to us, aren't they?" Archie whispered, his voice barely audible.

"Yup," Marci replied, "unless there's another group of kids hiding under these bushes."

Archie, completely petrified, lost his concentration and momentarily loosened his grip on Smokey. A moment was all Smokey needed. He wrestled free from Archie's relaxed grip and took off like a bullet toward the campfire.

Archie lunged after Smokey, but he was a second too slow to grab him. Archie could only lay there helplessly as Smokey left him lying in a heap in the grass.

Kay and Marci watched anxiously as Smokey rushed toward the men. Strangely enough, the men were completely unfazed by the charging dog. To everyone's amazement, when Smokey reached them, he ran through them as if they were holograms. He ran all about the campfire, chomping at the men, but his jaws caught nothing but air. It was as if they weren't really sitting there but were being projected onto the lawn.

As Smokey continued leaping about, one of the Union soldiers dipped a spoon into the pot hanging over the fire, ladled some gumbo into a bowl, and held it out. Smokey, who was as hungry as the children, suddenly stopped trying to attack them as he gratefully approached the man. He cautiously sniffed the bowl for a second before voraciously licking it clean and begging for more.

"Boy, you must be hungry," said the soldier. He dipped his spoon back into the pot and offered Smokey more. Within a matter of seconds, Smokey was sitting calmly at the soldier's side, devouring a second bowl of gumbo.

Kay described what she was seeing to Archie, who replied, "That's the craziest thing I've ever heard. Sometimes I wonder if you might be blind too."

"If she's blind, them so am I," Marci said, "because we're seeing the same thing."

As Smokey slurped up the Cajun stew, one of the Native Americans waved to the children.

"Come, join us, kids," he said. "If you're half as hungry as your dog, you'd be very foolish to keep your empty bellies lying on the ground under those bushes."

The children still weren't sure quite what to make of the strange men, but they seemed nice enough, and they had plenty of food. In the end, the children's aching stomachs won out over their scared minds, and they decided to accept the invitation. Kay went back and got Marci's chair for her, and then the children approached the campfire. As they did so, they could each see that a Union soldier was already ladling out bowls of gumbo for them.

Of the two Native Americans sitting around the fire, one wore a beaded headband with a goose feather hanging down the back and was a good deal older than his comrade. The three Union soldiers were very young, each no older than nineteen or twenty, and all three had bugle horn logos on their blue caps, indicating they were infantry soldiers. The two Confederate soldiers were both substantially older than the Union men, and their clothes were a little more threadbare and worn.

"Here y'all go." A Confederate soldier took the bowls from the Union soldier one by one and handed them to the children. "This here's my grandmama's recipe. If that ain't the best gumbo you've ever had, then I'll be a monkey's uncle."

Kay and Marci stared at their bowls of orange gumbo for a moment in an effort to determine whether it was real or not. Archie took in a deep breath of the aroma of the bowl, which certainly smelled real. Finally, they all dipped their spoons into the bowls and hesitantly took the first mouthfuls. The spicy broth, sausage, chicken, shrimp, and vegetables instantly made them want more. In less than a minute, all three bowls were empty. The children said nothing as they gathered beside the fire, greedily slurping down every last bit of broth.

"Want some more?" asked the Union soldier holding the ladle.

The children nodded. When they had all finished their second bowls just a few minutes later, there was an awkward moment of silence. The children looked around at this odd collection of men.

"You children look like you've seen a ghost," said the older Native American man.

This elicited a loud laugh from all the men around the campfire, and one of the Confederate soldiers almost choked on the wad of tobacco in his cheek. A Union soldier slapped him on the back, and within seconds, he'd coughed up the hunk of wet brown tobacco leaves.

"That, children, is one of the many reasons why you should

never chew tobacco," said the younger Native American man, shaking his head.

The children just smiled and nodded as they watched the Confederate soldier stuff another fistful of tobacco leaves into his mouth.

"Some people never learn," the young Native American man said with a grin.

"Sit down, kids," one of the Union soldiers said as he motioned Kay and Archie to an empty log on the opposite side of the fire.

Kay and Archie heeded his suggestion and seated themselves on the log. As they settled down, Marci addressed the older Native American man from her wheelchair.

"So, you said we look like we've seen a ghost. Have we?" she asked with a hesitant grin.

"No, don't be silly," the Native American warrior answered with a smile. "You children have not seen *a* ghost. By my count, you've seen seven." He gestured to the other six men around the fire.

The children gulped nervously. After a tense moment, Marci spoke.

"Come on," she said with a good-natured smile. "You guys are just Civil War reenactors, right?"

"Why would the two of us be dressed as Patawomeck warriors if we were here for a Civil War reenactment?" asked the older Native American.

Good question, the children thought.

"If you guys are ghosts, then how come you're petting Smokey and you were able to hand us those bowls of gumbo?" Marci asked.

"Spirits can touch whatever they want," the younger Native

American warrior replied. "But if we don't want something else to touch us, it can't."

Kay blurted out, "That sounds like a fairy tale to me."

The warrior picked up the ladle lying beside the pot of gumbo and handed it to Kay. Then he held his arm out, no less than a foot from where she sat.

"Hit my arm," he said.

Kay crinkled up her nose at him and said, "I'm not going to hit you."

"I wouldn't ask you to hit my arm if I thought you'd be able to do it," he replied with a grin. "Now, please hit my arm."

"Alright," Kay replied, "but I'm just going to tap it because I don't want to hurt you."

"I appreciate that," replied the Native American with a smile.

Kay raised the wooden ladle and slowly brought it down on the man's wrist. She braced herself for the slight impact, but she let out a tiny yelp when the ladle passed through the man's hand as if it wasn't even there and struck her on the knee. The children all stared in wonder at the ghostly man.

"So, you guys are all ghosts?" Marci asked as she looked at the circle of men.

They all nodded their heads.

"Boo!" said one of the Confederate soldiers, wiggling his arms over his head.

The other ghosts bellowed with laughter at this, while the children just smiled uneasily, not quite sure what to make of these strange beings. They certainly seemed nice enough—for ghosts.

"So, what brings you guys here?" Archie asked, his voice quivering slightly.

"We thought you would be able to answer that for us," the older Patawomeck warrior said. "Are you not the ones who called us here tonight?"

"I don't understand," Marci said. "You're here because someone called you?"

The soldiers just shrugged.

"I don't know why we're here," replied the Confederate soldier with the wad of tobacco in his mouth. "I'm just glad I got to eat Grandmama's gumbo again. It's been a hundred and fifty years too long."

"Everyone buried in this sacred ground was summoned by the spirits," replied the younger Patawomeck man. "We were summoned because someone is in search of the sacred Spearhead that has been guarded by our people for centuries. Are you not the ones in search of the Spearhead?"

"What would you say if we told you we *were* the ones in search of the Spearhead?" Archie asked with a nervous smile.

"I would say that the second piece of the Spearhead deserves to stay with my tribe. Why do you seek it?'"

"Because my brother is hurt," Marci said.

"I'm sorry to hear that," the Patawomeck warrior replied. "But what do you think the Spearhead can do for your brother?"

"Legend has it that the Spearhead possesses great powers," Marci said. "We want to use it to heal him."

The older Native warrior looked at his young compatriot and scratched his chin as he pondered Marci's words.

"The Spearhead is meant to be used by the Patawomeck," he finally said. "Is your brother a member of the Patawomeck Tribe?"

"He's not, but my sister and I are," Archie broke in.

"Then we may be related," the younger warrior said with a wink.

Kay smiled and began snapping her fingers at the thought that she might be in the presence of one of her ancestors. In fact, she thought the man had her mother's eyes—or maybe it was the other way around.

The elderly man took measure of the children for a long moment before speaking.

"I'm not so sure the Spearhead will be of any use to your friend," he said. "But if you two are members of our tribe, you may possess the second piece of the Spearhead, if you can find it."

"You mean the second piece isn't here?" Marci asked.

"No, it hasn't been here since construction of this fort began in 1861," the warrior replied. "When the colonizers built this fort, they desecrated and dug up many Patawomeck graves. It broke my heart to see the resting places of my friends and family being violated and moved like that. In fact, my young friend and I were the only Patawomeck whose burial sites survived the fort's construction. The second piece of the Spearhead had been hidden in the burial ground by the Patawomeck family that protected it. Fortunately, one of their descendants was able to dig it up and secure it elsewhere before construction started on this fort."

"Can you tell us where the Spearhead is now?" Archie asked.

"The Spearhead rests in the Federal City where the eagles fly high but no eagle dares walk," the warrior replied.

The children were flummoxed. It was obviously another riddle, but not one that made any sense to them.

"Can you tell us anything else?" Marci asked.

"If you're worthy, that's all the information you'll need."

"Thank you, sir," Marci replied. "I hope we are worthy."

"So do I," the old man replied. "But beware. The Spearhead is very valuable, and I sense there's a dark force following you to try and get their hands on it."

"I sense it too," said one of the Union soldiers. "Ghosts can't do much, but we *can* sense when someone's up to no good."

"Are you talking about the thief from the museum?" Marci asked.

"Not sure," said the younger Patawomeck warrior, "but I sense it pretty strongly myself." The Patawomeck warrior looked around the dark fort.

"You mean here in the park?" Marci asked.

"I don't know," the old man replied. "But I can sense it somewhere nearby."

Kay and Marci looked around to see if they could catch a glimpse of the mysterious thief from the museum, but as far as they could tell, no one else was in the park that night.

"Thank you for the warning," Marci said. "We'll be sure to keep an eye out for that guy as we continue our search."

The old Native American warrior nodded at her, then looked past her at Kay, who was raising her hand as if she were at school.

"Yes, young lady?" he said.

Kay pointed to the soldiers and said, "I have a question. I know you and your friend were buried here and the spirits summoned you, but how come the soldiers are here?"

"I was just wonderin' the same thing," said the Confederate soldier with the mouth full of tobacco.

"The spirits summoned everyone still buried in this ancient, sacred ground," replied the younger Patawomeck warrior. "These guys were buried here during the war, so the spirits summoned them as well."

"That's strange," Archie replied. "I thought there weren't any battles fought at Fort Ward."

"There weren't," replied one of the Union infantrymen. "The three of us were wounded at the First Battle of Bull Run in Manassas. We died from our wounds during the retreat back to Alexandria, and we were buried here."

"And the two of us was wounded and taken prisoner at the Battle of Antietam in Maryland," said the Confederate soldier with the tobacco in his mouth as he pointed to his Confederate comrade. "We both died of our wounds while they was bringing us back to Washington to be held in the Old Capitol Prison. When we passed away, they did us the honor of burying us in Southern soil, so they brung us 'cross the river and buried us right here next to these folks."

"I'm very sorry we disturbed you tonight," Archie said.

"Like I said before," said the talkative Confederate soldier, "'t'ain't no problem at all. If y'all hadn't disturbed us, I wouldn't've been able to enjoy this delicious gumbo again."

"Well, it's about the most delicious thing I've ever tasted," Archie replied. "And I'm not just saying that because I'm starving."

"I figured from the way y'all scarfed it down that ya hadn't eaten in a while," the soldier replied.

"And I ain't afraid to say you look a little tired too," added the other Confederate soldier. "Where are y'all plannin' on sleepin' tonight?"

"We were asleep over there by the cannons before we heard your harmonica," Marci said.

"Well, you can't sleep in the open air when we've got perfectly good tents right here for you," said one of the Union soldiers. "They haven't been used in over a century, but I'm sure it'll beat sleeping out here with all the bugs."

With those words, the ghosts set up three separate canvas tents for each of the children, along with pillows and blankets.

"Thank you," Marci said when they were done pitching the tents. "We could use a good night's sleep."

"It ain't the lap of luxury," said the Confederate soldier, "but it beats sleepin' in the grass."

As the children settled into their tents for some much-needed rest, they each wondered whether they would be able to fall asleep with a group of ghosts congregated right outside their tents. Much to their surprise, the ghosts had no intention of staying long.

"Children," said the older Patawomeck man, "I'm afraid our time has almost run out. Good luck on your quest!"

"Yeah, good luck, y'all!" said the chatty Confederate soldier.

Marci was about to ask where they were going, when the ghosts suddenly vanished, along with their entire campsite, save for the tents they had left for the children.

"They're gone!" Marci exclaimed.

Smokey, who had been lying in Marci's tent, rushed out and began barking and sniffing around the area where the men had been sitting just seconds before.

The other children sat in silence for a moment before Archie said, "Well, at least they left us their tents."

"This is hands-down the weirdest night of my life," Kay added.

The other children had to agree. Nevertheless, despite the evening's excitement, they were all exhausted and wanted nothing more than to get some sleep. Since the ghosts had warned them about dark forces, Kay volunteered to take the first shift as night watch to make sure no one snuck up on them in the darkness. While none of the other children were wild about the idea of sleeping inside tents that had been pitched by a group of ghosts, they were even less wild about the idea of sleeping completely exposed on the grass. So, despite their uneasiness, Marci and Archie were sound asleep in a matter of minutes. Kay tried her hardest to stay up and fulfill her duties as lookout, but she too was asleep a few minutes later, utterly exhausted from the events of the last few days.

As the children drifted off to sleep, they had no way of knowing that the dire warning of dark forces was absolutely true. In fact, just a few hundred yards away, in the trees, lurked the mysterious man in black, who was intent on retrieving the artifact the children had taken from him the previous night at the museum. Meanwhile, on the other side of the fence that separated Fort Ward from Van Dorn Street, sat Agent Nighthawk, who once again kept vigil over the children as they slept. Neither the agent nor the thief dared approach the children's campsite, as they had seen a group of men with the children and assumed the strange fellows were still around somewhere. But both men kept watch, content to resume their hunt in the morning.

The next morning at seven o'clock, Park Ranger Jimmy Wyatt began his day as he always did by driving his truck around the fort to make sure nothing was amiss. In nearly twenty years on the job, he'd rarely found anything aside from the occasional case of minor vandalism, like an overturned trash can or bit of spray paint on one of the cannons. But as he drove past the Northwest Bastion that morning, he saw something that was usually only reserved for those days when a Civil War reenactment was scheduled to take place: a campsite. He stopped his truck and rubbed his eyes to make sure he wasn't seeing things, but sure enough, there in front of him on the lawn were three canvas tents, just like those used by the Civil War reenactors when they were in town.

"What is that about?" he muttered to himself. He grabbed his park calendar from the glove box to see if there was a reenactment scheduled for this weekend that he had forgotten about. As he suspected, no reenactments were planned until October.

Ranger Wyatt put his calendar back in the glove box, parked his truck, and got out to investigate the mysterious tents. The arthritis in his knees caused him to wince as he descended from the truck.

"Hey!" he called as he slowly made his way across the expanse of green grass that lay in front of the fort's Northwest Bastion.

The children were all so exhausted, they would have been hard pressed to wake up even if an explosion had gone off in the park. Smokey, on the other hand, had already begun to stir at the sound of Ranger Wyatt's truck. The ranger's voice as he approached was enough to send Smokey scurrying from the tent he shared with Marci.

"A dog?" Ranger Wyatt said as he saw Smokey emerge from one of the tents. "What's going on here?"

As the ranger walked closer, Smokey sensed he needed to get the children out of the park, and in a hurry. He began barking furiously, but none of them moved. Smokey then poked his head into Marci's tent and began pulling on her shoelaces to rouse her.

"Leave me alone. I'm tired," Marci said as she tried to roll over.

Smokey only pulled harder, until Marci finally sat up and looked around. She instantly realized it was morning, and a sudden panic swept over her. She crawled out of the tent and saw an older man in a park ranger's uniform approaching at a determined limp.

"Wake up! Wake up! Wake up!" Marci yelled as she pulled herself over to her wheelchair.

Luckily, between Smokey's barking and Marci's yelling, the other children awoke in an instant.

"Come on!" Marci yelled. "We have to get out of here!"

"What do you kids think you're doing here?" Ranger Wyatt cried as he approached.

Thanks to Ranger Wyatt's knee problems, the children had no trouble getting to Kay and Archie's bike before he was upon them. In a matter of seconds, they were back out on Braddock Road.

"Where are we headed?" Kay yelled at Marci as they made their way west on Braddock Road.

"I don't know," Marci replied. "Any ideas?"

"Let's go to the library," Archie replied. "I think we're going to need to do some research to figure out that last clue."

Beatley Library on Duke Street was only a couple miles away. Since it wouldn't open for another hour, the kids decided to stop off first at the supermarket and buy breakfast. With only $8.85 left, they had to be especially frugal. They bought two apples to split amongst them, an eight-ounce bottle of water for each of them, and some cold cuts for Smokey to munch on.

"We're just about out of money," Kay said. As they sat on a bench outside the library, she used a boxcutter from her tool belt to cut the apples into slices they could share.

The others were all trying to ignore the growling sounds coming from their stomachs as they ate their meager breakfasts. As usual, they shared enough with Smokey that he ended up eating and drinking more than anyone.

"We've got to find the Spearhead today," Archie said. "We can't keep this up much longer."

"We will," Marci replied. "I've got a good feeling about that last clue."

"Do you know what it means?" Archie asked.

"No, I'm afraid I don't," she admitted. "But how many places can there be in DC where eagles fly high but no eagle dares walk?"

"The zoo is the only place I can think of where there's an eagle in DC," Kay said.

"Yeah, I think that should be the first place we go," Archie said.

"Well, not so fast," Kay said. "We might find something in the library that points us in another direction."

○○○

Unfortunately, when the library doors opened thirty minutes later, the children weren't able to uncover anything that made the clue any clearer. They thumbed through every book they could find on eagles, but none of them had the slightest thing to do with Washington, DC. As for the books on Washington, DC, none of them said much of anything about eagles aside from a couple references to prominent eagle statues in the city, including the one at the World War I memorial near the Treasury Department on Pennsylvania Avenue and another in Statuary Hall in the Capitol. When they sat down at one of the computers to do an internet search for the terms "eagle" and "Washington, DC," they got nothing but websites for various businesses. After three hours of mostly fruitless research, Marci decided they should get going before the entire day slipped away.

"I don't think we're going to be able to find anything else," she said. "I say we go to the zoo first, then we check out those statues at the war memorial and the Capitol if we can't find anything at the zoo."

"Sounds good," Archie said. "I guess we've gotta ride all the way to the zoo since we've got almost no money left?"

"Yup," Kay said. "We've only got enough money for one of us to get there and back on the Metro."

"I guess we should get going then," Marci said. "We've got a long ride ahead of us."

Kay searched online for directions to the zoo, from there to the World War I memorial, and from there to the Capitol Building. Once she'd written those down in her notebook, they were off.

OOO

Two hours later, at one o'clock in the afternoon, they arrived at the zoo on Connecticut Avenue in DC. Smokey had been unable to keep up after several miles and spent the rest of the trip in Marci's lap. They were exhausted from the long, hot ride, but when they finally arrived, they were so exhilarated at the thought of finding the second piece of the Spearhead that they wasted no time finding the eagles. They rode past the panda habitat and then around the Elephant House. After the Elephant House, they took a sharp right past the otter habitat before arriving in a part of the zoo known as Valley Trail.

"There they are," Kay said as she looked up at the two bald eagles who made their home in the Eagle Refuge. They were both perched near each other atop a rock formation that overlooked a manmade waterfall.

As the children looked up, Marci made an observation that caused each of their hearts to sink.

"Look at that netting," she said, referring to the enclosure that covered the entire refuge. "It doesn't look to me like these eagles can fly very high."

"Actually, these two eagles can't fly at all," Kay added.

"What do you mean?" Marci asked.

"Check it out," Kay said as she pointed to the text on the placard in front of the refuge and read it aloud for Archie.

According to the placard, Sam, the female eagle, was missing the tip of her left wing due to a gunshot wound she'd suffered in Alaska. Tioga, the male, had been found near his Pennsylvania nest as a fledgling. A wildlife rehabilitator determined he had a fractured left shoulder that had healed in a bad position and made it impossible for him to fly. Since neither eagle could fly to take care of themselves, they had been brought to the zoo.

"These eagles can't fly high at all," Kay said. "The riddle doesn't make a whole lot of sense if this is the place."

"Alright," Marci announced, "it's pretty clear this isn't the right place. Should we go to the war memorial or the Capitol?"

"According to the directions I found online, the war memorial is closer," Kay said.

"Alright, so long, Sam and Tioga!" Marci announced as she turned her chair and began wheeling back to the front of the zoo. She was trying her best to stay chipper so the others didn't get too down, but on the inside, she was sorely disappointed.

Once they left the zoo, they rode down Connecticut Avenue, made their way over to Fifteenth Street, and headed due south until they arrived at the World War I memorial. The memorial was catty-corner to the Treasury building and directly across the street from the famous Willard Hotel, where Abe Lincoln stayed before his first inauguration and Dr. Martin Luther King put the finishing touches on his "I Have a Dream" speech. At the west end of the memorial was a statue known as the "Bex Eagle." The Bex Eagle depicted an eagle with its wings outspread and one set of talons resting on a sculpture of the Earth with the other set outstretched as if reaching for prey.

When the children arrived at the memorial, they stood at the base of the statue for a few moments. Kay described the statue to Archie, and he touched it with his hands to get a better sense of what it depicted. They hoped the answer to the riddle would suddenly come to them. Unfortunately, it didn't.

"I don't get it," Marci announced.

"Me neither," Archie added.

"This eagle is definitely flying high," Kay said. "And he has one foot on the top of the Earth and the other reaching out and grabbing for something."

"Okay," Archie replied, "but how does that help solve the riddle?"

"He's got one foot on the North Pole and the other foot would probably come down on Russia." Kay's forehead crinkled as she studiously scratched her chin. "So, this is telling us that the eagle flies high over the North Pole but doesn't dare walk in Russia."

"What on earth does that mean?" Archie asked.

Kay stared at him for a moment before saying, "I have no idea."

"That can't be right," Marci said. "How can the Spearhead be at the North Pole and in Russia?"

"There are three pieces, remember?" Kay said. "Maybe it means the second piece is in the North Pole and the final piece is in Russia."

"Well, I hope that's not right," Archie said. "We don't have money for the Metro, much less a trip to the North Pole and then Russia. Anyone else have any other guesses about what this statue means, or should we head off to the Capitol?"

No one said anything.

"Alright, then it's off to the Capitol!" Archie announced.

Luckily, the Capitol was just a short ride down Pennsylvania Avenue. In order to enter the Capitol, they had to go through the Capitol Visitor Center, which was located on the East Front of the Capitol Building. As the children arrived at the East Front, the man in black who had been following them all day took out his cell phone and made a call.

"Sir, you ain't going to believe this, but they're right outside your door," he said.

"What do you mean?" said the voice on the other line.

"I mean they're going into the Capitol right now. The Visitor Center, East Front."

"What are they doing here?" the voice on the other line asked excitedly.

"I dunno," the man said. "But I don't think I can follow them in. The kids might recognize me from the other night."

The man on the other line was no longer there—he had already hung up the phone and dashed out of his office on his way down to the Capitol Visitor Center.

Meanwhile, Agent Nighthawk was also still keeping an eye on the children, but unlike the man in black, he decided to follow the children into the Capitol.

The children had locked up their bike and entered the Visitor Center. They still had no idea they were being followed by either the mysterious man in black or Agent Nighthawk. Even so, these two men were the least of their worries. They were suddenly confronted with an obstacle they hadn't planned for: they needed tickets to actually get inside the Capitol Building.

"We need a ticket to get inside!" Marci exclaimed as she stared at a sign in front of the passageway to the Capitol.

"What'll we do?" Archie asked. "We don't have any tickets!"

"What will you do?" asked a tall, older man in a blue pin-striped suit.

Kay and Marci caught their breath as they stared up in awe at the smartly dressed man. He looked vaguely familiar, but neither of them could remember where they had seen him before. Archie also thought he recognized the voice, but he couldn't quite place it.

"If only you had a member of Congress who could arrange to give you a tour," the man said with a wide grin.

"I'm sorry, sir," Marci began to say. "But we—"

"Well, as luck would have it," the man said, "I just happen to know a senator who can help you."

Archie crinkled up his forehead and said, "Your voice sounds very familiar. Have I heard you on the news?"

"Perhaps," the man replied with a grin. "Hey, that's an awfully cute service dog you have there."

"Thanks! His name's Smokey," Archie said.

"Wait—you're Senate Majority Leader Lucius Maxwell!" Kay exclaimed.

A small crowd had already begun to gather as people recognized the senator, but after Kay's outburst, most everyone near the entrance of the Visitor Center began to make their way over to ask for an autograph or just to gawk.

"Folks, I'm very sorry." The senator held up his hands to get the crowd's attention. "But I'm here to give a tour to my friends here. I'm afraid I don't have any time for autographs." Then, looking at the children, he said, "Shall we get started?"

The children nodded and gladly followed the senator as he led them into the Capitol.

Marci and the others each began to wonder if they were dreaming. How could it be that the senate majority leader would come along to give them a tour of the Capitol at the very moment they realized they weren't going to able to get in without tour tickets? It seemed almost too good to be true.

"Thank you so much, Senator," Marci said. "We didn't realize we'd need tickets to get in."

"It's my pleasure," the senator replied. "I just happened to be passing through the Visitor Center when I heard you say you didn't have any tickets, and it broke my heart."

"Well, we definitely appreciate it," Archie added.

"Do you think we can go to Statuary Hall?" Kay blurted out, snapping her fingers rapidly.

"Of course," the senator said. "Any particular reason you want to get there first?"

"Oh, no," Marci said quickly, "we just heard about it in school and wanted to see it in person."

"We've really been looking forward to it," Archie added. He switched the bag that carried the first piece of the Spearhead from one shoulder to the other.

"Would you like me to carry that bag for you, young man?" the senator asked. "It looks awfully heavy."

"Oh, no thank you," he replied. "It's not heavy."

"Are you sure?" The senator reached for the bag with a grin. "I can't let you carry such a heavy bag all by yourself."

"It actually has my medicine in it," Archie fibbed. "I need to keep it with me at all times."

"Oh," the senator replied, pursing his lips and furrowing his brow in annoyance. He took his hand off the strap over Archie's shoulder as they entered the large semicircular room south of the Capitol Rotunda known as Statuary Hall.

"Well, here we are, children," the senator said as they entered the grand hall. "This room was the meeting place of the U.S. House of Representatives for nearly fifty years, until the House chamber was built in 1857. Now it's an art gallery for some of the most famous statues in America."

"Do you know which one has the eagle?" Kay asked, her fingers still snapping away. She was as nervous as ever to speak to a stranger like the senator, but her impatience to find the Spearhead overtook her nerves.

"Excuse me?" the senator asked.

"She loves eagles," Marci added. "Do you know if there are any eagle statues?"

The senator smiled. "As a matter of fact, the most prominent statue in the hall is called 'Liberty and the Eagle.' It's that one right over there. Follow me."

As the children followed the senator across the hall, Kay and Marci stared up at the imposing sculpture of an American eagle with both wings outspread. The eagle sat to the right of a woman who was standing with a scroll in her right hand.

"Who's that lady?" Kay asked after she'd described the statue for Archie.

"That's Lady Liberty," the senator replied, "and that scroll in her right hand is the Constitution. This is one of my favorite statues."

As the children stood in front of the sculpture, their hearts sank. This statue of an eagle was neither flying nor walking. Instead, this eagle had their wings spread as if they were about to take off, but both talons were planted firmly on the ground. The children realized the statue did nothing to solve the riddle.

"What's the matter, children?" the senator asked. "You seem disappointed."

The children simply stood in sad silence before the statue.

"I didn't know you were such art critics," the senator remarked. "Why don't we look at some of the other pieces? I'm sure there's something in here that you'll like."

"Senator," Marci said, "thanks so much for showing us around, but I think it's time for us to get home."

"But we just started our tour!" he exclaimed. "You can't leave now!"

"I know, sir, we're very sorry, but we really ought to get going," Marci said. "Thanks again for your help."

"Well, where do you live? How are you getting home?" the senator asked.

"We're going to ride home to Alexandria," Kay said.

"Ride to Alexandria!" the senator exclaimed. "That's madness! Here, come up to my office, and I'll arrange for a driver to take you home."

"Oh no, we couldn't," Marci said.

"Nonsense." The senator spread out his arms and began herding the children out of the hall. "Come, we have a special elevator for senators."

As they left the hall, the senator placed his hand on Archie's shoulder strap and said with a smile, "Young man, I'm going to have to insist on carrying this heavy bag for you."

Before Archie could say a word, the senator deftly snatched the bag from his arm and clutched it tightly in his hands. Kay and Marci exchanged nervous glances as the senator grasped the bag that contained the first piece of the Spearhead.

"You just let me know if you need that medicine, and I'll give this right back," the senator said.

"Okay," Archie replied with a nervous smile.

They walked behind the senator toward a bank of elevators, and Marci whispered to Kay, "I've got a bad feeling about this guy."

"Me too," Kay replied. "Why's he so interested in getting his hands on that bag?"

"I think we need to get out of here," Marci said. "I have an idea." She leaned over and whispered in Kay's ear.

Kay then leaned over and whispered the same thing to Archie. They arrived at the elevators just as one was opening.

"Well, how's that for timing!" the senator exclaimed.

After a few stuffy-looking men and women exited the elevator and exchanged pleasantries with the senator, he turned to the children and beckoned them on board.

Once they were all inside the elevator, the senator pressed the button to send the elevator up to his office.

Marci exclaimed, "Now!"

Archie and Kay turned around and kicked the senator in the shins.

"Ouch!" The senator dropped Archie's bag while he clutched at his throbbing legs. The bag never even had a chance to hit the floor. Marci reached out, grabbed it, and quickly followed Kay, Archie, and Smokey out of the elevator.

The senator was still doubled over in pain when he screamed, "Stop those kids! Stop those ki—" But before he could finish, the doors to the elevator slid shut, and the children and Smokey sped out of the Capitol as fast as they could.

16

The children pedaled furiously away from the Capitol with Smokey, as usual, running alongside them.

"Where are we headed?" Kay called out to Marci.

"Union Station!" she replied.

"Why are we going there?" Archie asked.

"Because there are tons of people there!" Marci said. "I want to be in the most public place possible in case the senator comes after us!"

Marci was wise to choose Union Station, because at that moment, the senator was on his cell phone ordering his mysterious henchman to follow the children. Agent Nighthawk, of course, was also close on their heels as they pedaled to the fountain in front of historic Union Station, the train station that sits adjacent to the U.S. Capitol.

"Boy, that guy was creepy!" Archie said as they stopped in front of the fountain.

"You're telling me!" Kay said. "He was determined to get that bag from you."

"Yeah, it was almost like he knew the Spearhead was in the bag," Marci said.

"I think he did," Archie replied. "He sure wanted to get his hands on it."

"Well, I'm glad we got out of there," Kay said. "I just wish we had gotten closer to finding the second piece of the Spearhead."

Just as it began to dawn on Marci that their search was over and they had failed, Archie heard a distant chant that lifted his spirits.

"Do you guys hear that?" Archie asked, a grin slowly growing across his face.

"No," Kay said, "what is it?"

"Just listen," Archie said.

A moment passed before Kay and Marci heard anything. But sure enough, as they concentrated, they eventually heard the distinct sound of voices chanting in the distance. The children could just barely hear the word "eagle."

"I hear it," Marci said. "Where's it coming from?"

"Over there," Archie replied as he pointed down North Capitol Street. Marci looked in that direction and saw a bell tower looming in the distance.

"Well, let's go check it out!" Kay said.

As the group rode up North Capitol Street, the chanting grew louder.

"Eagles fly high! Eagles fly high!"

Minutes later, the children arrived at the base of the bell tower. It was connected to a large church named for Saint Aloysius Gonzaga that sat beside a football field on the grounds of Gonzaga High School, the oldest school in Washington, DC.

As the children pulled up to the church, Kay and Marci were able to see the source of the chanting. The football team was gathered on the field and finishing practice with a series of sprints. As the team finished each sprint, they chanted, "Eagles fly high! Eagles fly high!"

At the corner of Eye Street and North Capitol Street stood

the gate to Gonzaga High School, atop which sat a large sculpture of an eagle in flight. The practice jerseys that the football team wore were emblazoned with the words "Gonzaga Eagles."

Kay told Archie where they were and described the team's jerseys.

"Are you guys thinking what I'm thinking?" Marci said.

Kay looked at her with a raised eyebrow and said, "This could just be a coincidence."

"Yeah," Marci said, "or it could be the break we've been looking for."

"But why would the Spearhead be hidden at a high school?" Archie asked.

"I have no idea," Marci said, "but I plan to find out."

She started wheeling her chair up Eye Street toward the main building of the school. Kay, Archie, and Smokey fell in line behind her. As they made their way up Eye Street, they noticed that a number of students were coming and going from a building that said "Dooley Hall" across the front door. School was not in session yet, but summer school was just winding down. Dooley Hall was the main building on the nearly two-hundred-year-old campus, and a sign by the front door indicated that it housed a chapel, library, administrative offices, the school theater, and some classrooms.

"Come on," Marci said, "let's go inside and check it out."

As they made their way into Dooley Hall, Archie dutifully attached Smokey's collar and once again pretended he was his service dog.

Upon entering Dooley Hall, they saw the school's small chapel straight ahead. It seemed as good a place as any to start their search, but as Marci rolled toward the chapel, she heard someone yell, "What do you think you're doing?"

Startled, she turned and saw an older boy, presumably one of the students at the high school, walking toward her.

"I said, what are you doing?" the older boy repeated.

"Uh, just looking around," Marci replied. "Sorry, I didn't mean to upset anyone."

"Get off the seal!" the older boy bellowed as he towered over her.

Marci was too confused to know what to do, so all she could muster as a response was, "What?"

"Get off the seal!" the boy repeated. "You're right on top of the school seal!"

Marci looked down. Beneath her chair's wheels was a circular mosaic in the floor that depicted an eagle with its wings outstretched over a coat of arms, encircled by the Latin words "Collegium Gonzagaeum Washingtoniense."

"Oh, I'm sorry." Marci rolled her chair off the seal. "Won't happen again."

"Sheesh," the older boy said as he started to walk away. "Some people."

As the boy made his way down the hall, Archie peeled himself away from the wall where he and Kay had been cowering and said, "Um, excuse me, but can I ask you a question?"

The older boy stopped in his tracks, sighed heavily, and turned around. "What?" he snapped.

"Umm, well, why did you tell Marci to get off the seal?" he asked.

"Because it's been a tradition for over a hundred and fifty years that no one crosses the school seal," the boy said. "Any other questions?"

"Umm, nope, thank you," Archie said.

Once the older boy had walked to the end of the long

hall and was out of sight, Kay said, "The Spearhead rests in the Federal City where the eagles fly high, but no eagle dares walk."

"We're in the Federal City," Archie said.

"And this is where the eagles fly high," Marci added.

"And that is where no eagle dares walk," Kay said with a smile as she pointed at the school seal on the floor.

"I think we've got to find a way to get under that school seal," Marci said. Then she looked at Kay and said, "Anything in your tool belt that could help with that?"

Kay removed the small hammer and screwdriver from their slots in the belt. "I think these'll do the trick."

"We just need to find out how you can get to work on the seal when no one's around," Marci said.

Even though it was late in the afternoon, there were still some students and teachers milling about, so there was no way that Kay could start hammering away at the seal without causing a scene.

"We're going to have wait until the building's empty," Marci said. "We just need to find a place to hide out in here until everyone leaves."

"Do you have any place in mind?" Archie asked.

"I do," Marci said as she fixed her gaze on the school chapel.

The chapel could hold fifty people, but on that summer afternoon, it was completely empty and silent. At the north end was a small altar, and along the western wall were two confessionals.

"We could hide in the confessionals," Marci said.

"Do we have to?" Kay scrunched up her face.

"Do you have any other ideas?" Marci asked.

They all looked around the chapel for someplace other than the small confessionals to hide in, but they saw no better options.

Marci rolled into one confessional and held Smokey in her lap, while Kay and Archie sat cramped in the other. For the better part of three hours, they waited for the sun to go down outside and the last inhabitants of Dooley Hall to go home for the evening. By the time the nightly cleaning crew had come through and vacuumed the chapel, mopped the floors of Dooley Hall, and turned out all the lights in the building, the children felt it was finally safe to emerge from their close quarters.

"Oh, thank goodness that's over," Kay said as she emerged from the confessional and collapsed on the floor. "You really need a shower," she said to her brother.

"You don't exactly smell great either, and my sense of smell is stronger than yours, so imagine how awful that was for me," he said.

"Alright guys," Marci said, "let's focus. We've got a job to finish."

With those words, the children and Smokey moved quietly to the chapel door. The only light in the chapel was the moonlight seeping in through the windows, but it was more than enough for the children to easily find their way.

Marci opened the chapel door and slowly wheeled herself out, looking up and down the hall to see if anyone was around, but the building appeared to be deserted. She motioned for the others to follow her, then made her way over to the seal.

"Are you ready to do this?" Marci asked Kay.

Kay had already removed the hammer and screwdriver from her belt, but she paused.

"What if the Spearhead isn't under there?" she said. "Then I'll have destroyed this seal for nothing."

"But what if it is under there?" Archie said. "Don't we have a duty to our Tribe to find out?"

"And what about Hector?" Marci said. "This is our last hope of saving him."

"You're right," Kay said. Then she knelt down and placed the screwdriver against the mosaic tiles in the floor. She started to raise the hammer to take her first strike at the seal—when a tall, slender figure emerged from the shadows.

"I wouldn't do that if I were you," whispered the dark figure.

The children froze in terror.

"It's much easier if you just do this," said the mysterious man. He reached up and placed his hand on a sculpture of an eagle's head that jutted out of the wall beside the chapel door, then turned it counterclockwise ninety degrees. The seal in the floor slid away, revealing a shiny stone object lying in the empty space in the floor.

"Oh my goodness," Marci said. She and the others stared open-mouthed at what they were certain was the second piece of the Spearhead.

"Is that what you've been looking for?" The man stepped closer and allowed the children to finally see his face.

He was a priest, as evidenced by his black suit and white collar. He had thick black hair interspersed with shocks of gray, a deeply wrinkled face, and pale blue eyes. He leaned over Kay, who was still kneeling beside the hole in the floor, and reached in to grab the second piece of the Spearhead.

As he pulled it out and grasped it in his hand, he said, "So, which one of you would like this?"

Archie was the first to speak up. "You're—you're—you're just going to give it to us?" he asked.

"My duty is to safeguard the Spearhead, but if someone from the Patawomeck Tribe comes in search of it, my duty is to assist them. I overheard you say that you are members of the Tribe, is that right?"

Kay nodded. "Yes, my brother and I are Patawomeck."

"And it sounds like you need it to save someone?" he asked.

"Yes, my brother is in the hospital, and no one can figure out how to make him better," Marci said.

"Then this belongs to you," the priest said. He handed the second piece of the Spearhead to Kay, who gratefully accepted it.

"Thank you," she said, staring in wonder at the glistening piece of quartz.

"Can I ask you a question?" Archie said to the priest.

"Of course," the priest replied.

"What is the second piece of the Spearhead doing here in this school?"

"Good question," the priest replied with a smile. "This piece of the Spearhead was removed from the ancient burial ground during the construction of Fort Ward by a descendant of the Patawomeck family who has protected the Spearhead for centuries. That descendant also happened to be a Jesuit priest who taught at Gonzaga and eventually became the school's president. Since all Jesuit priests take a vow of poverty, he thought hiding the second piece of the Spearhead with his Jesuit brothers would ensure its safety. They could be trusted to guard the Spearhead without being tempted to use it for their own selfish purposes. Ever since then, each president of this school has been entrusted with its protection."

"So, I guess you're Mr. President?" Marci asked.

"I am," the priest replied. "But there's no need to call me Mr. President. Father Longtin will do just fine."

"Okay, Father Longtin," Archie said, "I've got another question for you: where can the spirit be heard?"

Father Longtin scrunched up his face and cocked his head sideways, not quite sure what to make of the question.

"Well, I'm a priest," Father Longtin replied with a smile. "I can think of any number of places one might hear the spirit."

"I'm talking about the spirit in this riddle: 'He who searches for the Patawomeck head of the spear need not look far, for the first piece is near. It rests among those relics that traveled with the great man when liberty stood in the valley and darkness was at hand. When the first piece is found, there is still yet another, but to find it, one must go where the Patawomeck lie next to their brothers. If the sojourner finds them, the spirit must be heard, for none other than she can reveal the third.'"

"So, you want to know where the 'spirit must be heard' so you can find the third piece of the Spearhead?" Father Longtin asked.

"Exactly," Archie replied.

Father Longtin sighed and shrugged. "I'm afraid I don't have the foggiest idea, but I suspect the answer may lie in the two pieces of the Spearhead that you already have."

As Kay pulled the first piece of the Spearhead from her bag, the two pieces suddenly flew out of her hands and snapped together as though magnetized. There was a sharp noise like cracking ice, and the entire room was briefly illuminated as if by a bolt of lightning. Archie jumped back, while the others threw their hands up to shield their eyes. When they lowered them, blinking back spots, what they saw amazed them.

Lying on the floor was a single, large piece of quartz with

several words emblazoned on it, which Kay, bending to pick it up, read aloud: "The spirit resides where freedom abides and the Spearhead's protectors made their home."

"Well," Father Longtin said with a laugh, "it looks like you got your clue. Does it mean anything to you?"

"I'm afraid not," Marci replied as she looked quizzically at the words.

"I know what they mean," Kay said with a grin. "I know exactly what they mean!" She turned to Father Longtin and was so overcome with excitement that she said, "Thanks for all your help, Father. I know where we need to go now to find the final piece of the Spearhead."

"That's wonderful," replied Father Longtin. "I'd be happy to give you a ride wherever you're going so long as you don't mind having an old man tag along."

"A ride would be great," Kay said, "but only if you have a boat."

"A boat!" Father Longtin replied. "Where in heaven's name are you going?"

"Freedom Island," Kay replied. "It's an island in the Potomac near Mount Vernon where the Patawomeck family that protected the Spearhead settled."

"Of course!" Marci exclaimed.

"Was that Freedom Island, you said?" came a strangely familiar, raspy voice.

A dark figure emerged from the shadow of a pillar. Before anyone could react, he darted forward, snatched the Spearhead off the ground, and dashed for the main entrance. As the doors flew open, Marci glimpsed the figure's face in the orange light of the street lamps: it was the man in black from the museum.

"It's the guy from the museum!" she exclaimed.

Once they overcame their shock, the children and Smokey took off after the man. They were hopeful that Smokey would be able to intercept him outside, just as he had done at the museum.

By the time the children and Smokey made their way out of Dooley Hall, it was too late. The man was already climbing into the back seat of a black Mercedes with a U.S. Senate license plate. As the car sped off down Eye Street and veered sharply onto North Capitol, Kay and Marci distinctly saw the dark visage of Senator Maxwell grinning back at them through the rear window.

"The burglar is with the senator! He must work for him!" Marci exclaimed.

"Come, children, we haven't a moment to lose!" said Father Longtin, who had just emerged from Dooley Hall.

"Where are we going to go?" Archie replied. "The senator and his lackey are off to Freedom Island, and we have no way to get there."

"You said you needed a boat, didn't you?" Father Longtin asked.

"Yes," Archie answered.

"Well, I think I know where we can find one," Father Longtin replied.

17

Kay was in the front seat of Father Longtin's car, and the other children and Smokey were in the back seat. Father Longtin was talking on his cell phone as he drove, which was something he never did, as it was unsafe, but these were extraordinary circumstances.

"Yes, Coach Lewis, I need you to meet me at the boathouse in ten minutes," Father Longtin said. "I don't have time to explain, I just need you to get down there with a key to the speed boat." He paused for a moment. "Excellent, I'll see you there in a few minutes."

"Is everything alright?" Marci asked.

"Yes," Father Longtin replied. "That was the coach of my school's crew team. He's going to meet us at the boathouse and give me the keys to his speedboat."

Father Longtin pulled off the freeway at the Navy Yard exit, and in a matter of minutes, they were at the Anacostia Boathouse at Eleventh and O Streets.

As they pulled into the parking lot, there was a lone man there leaning against the trunk of a car. He wore a white windbreaker with the words "Gonzaga Crew" on the breast.

After climbing out of Father Longtin's car and retrieving Marci's wheelchair from the trunk, they approached the man.

"Hey, Father," said the man.

"Hello, Coach Lewis," Father Longtin said. "I appreciate you meeting me here at this unholy hour."

"No problem at all," Coach Lewis replied. "I don't live too far away." He gave the children and their dog a puzzled look. "I didn't realize you were running a daycare these days."

Father Longtin smiled and said, "Yes, this is a bit odd. Perhaps I can explain all of this to you later, but if you don't mind, I'd very much like to get to the speed boat. This is an emergency."

"Uh, sure," Coach Lewis replied. "Follow me."

Father Longtin and the children followed the coach to the boathouse, where he unlocked the doors and led them to the docks. At the end of the dock was an old speed boat that Coach Lewis used to monitor the varsity and junior varsity crew teams.

As he took the vinyl cover off the boat, Coach Lewis said, "It's not real fast, but it runs well, and it's got a full tank of gas. Where are you headed?"

"Down to Mount Vernon," Father Longtin replied. "Do we have enough gas to get that far?"

"Oh, sure," Coach Lewis replied. "There's not much down by Mount Vernon, though."

"Yes, mostly just some islands," Father Longtin said as he took the keys from Coach Lewis. "Thank you very much, Coach. I promise to return your boat without a scratch by morning."

"Well, since you're the president of the school, it's really your boat," Coach Lewis replied. "You can bring it back whenever you like. Have you ever been behind the wheel of a speed boat?"

"Yes, I grew up on the Chesapeake Bay, so I learned how to drive a boat before I could drive a car. Now, come, children." Father Longtin reached into a compartment in the floor of the boat and pulled out three life vests. "You'll each need to put one of these on."

Once everyone had put on their vests, Father Longtin fired up the engine, bade farewell to Coach Lewis, and sped out of the dock as fast as the boat would carry them.

The Anacostia River flowed from Prince George's County, Maryland, through Washington, DC, where it emptied into the Potomac River. In a matter of minutes, Father Longtin had guided them onto the Potomac and past National Airport toward Alexandria.

As the boat sped past Alexandria, the children stared at the lights that shone atop the Masonic Temple at the center of the city. It was difficult for any of them to believe that just two nights before, they had been balancing precariously on a ledge outside that building, wondering if they would live to tell the tale.

Staring at the lights of Alexandria, it occurred to each of them that at the west end of the city, Hector was still lying helpless in his hospital bed. When they'd started their quest, they'd been so confident it would end successfully. Tonight, they'd had success in the palm of their hands, only to have it taken away. Now they were speeding off in the hope that they could regain the Spearhead, but none of them were confident. Senator Maxwell had a good head start on them, and there was no telling what he would do if he got his hands on the third piece of the Spearhead before the children got to the island.

After passing Alexandria, the boat motored on for several miles before the lights of the mansion at Mount Vernon came into view on a ridge overlooking the river. General Washington's home shone like a beacon, indicating that Freedom Island was close.

"It would be best to cut the engine and paddle in so the senator doesn't hear us coming," Father Longtin said to the children over the roar of the engine, "but I'm afraid we don't have time for that. I think we need to motor in at full speed."

"I think you're right," Marci said. "We don't have a second to spare."

Within minutes, the dark silhouette of Freedom Island came into view in the distance, as did the ominous outline of a large speed boat docked against the rocks.

"That's got to be the senator's boat," Marci announced.

Father Longtin spotted a patch of sandy beachfront not too far from the senator's boat, guided their boat ashore, and only cut the engine when the water was shallow enough him for him to throw the anchor overboard and jump out after it. He helped Marci climb out and onto his back while the other children and Smokey jumped into the knee-deep water and ran ashore.

"Do you hear that chanting?" Kay asked.

"Yeah, it's coming from over there." Archie pointed inland, toward the dark woods at the center of the island.

"Only one way to find out what's going on." Kay headed in the direction of the chanting, grasping Archie's hand. Father Longtin followed close behind with Marci on his back.

As they moved farther into the woods, the chanting grew louder until a flash of light rose above the forest and illuminated a small clearing in the woods. Standing in the middle of the clearing was a tall, slender man wearing a bright red robe with a white sash. He was holding the two merged pieces of the Spearhead over his head. Standing next to him was the senator's henchman, the man in black. As the mysterious light reached its apex in the sky, it illuminated the face of the man in the red robe—Senator Maxwell.

"Senator Maxwell must have been the one we saw leading the chanting at the Masonic Temple the other night," Marci said. Archie and Kay nodded in agreement.

The children were still too far away to hear what the senator was saying, but they could see that something was descending from the light that shone above the forest.

"That light is the spirit," Father Longtin said with a look of horror on his face. "It's giving the senator the final piece of the Spearhead."

"No!" Kay screamed. She ran out from the woods toward the senator, hoping to snatch the Spearhead out of the senator's hands before he could incorporate the final piece.

But it was hopeless. The senator's henchman grabbed Kay before she could get within ten feet of the Spearhead.

"That belongs to my tribe!" she yelled. "You have no right to it!"

"You're too late!" the senator proclaimed triumphantly. The third piece of the Spearhead floated toward him and merged with the other pieces. He held the complete Spearhead aloft and stared at it greedily as it lit up the dark night.

"Your tribe has wasted the Spearhead's potential all these years," the senator proclaimed. "I'll sell it to a drug company and make a fortune!"

Kay struggled to wrestle herself free from the henchman's grip, but he was stronger than her. She sobbed uncontrollably out of frustration and sadness that her tribe's Spearhead had been found by someone whose only intention was to sell it.

Archie could hear his sister's cries and longed to go to her. He and Marci both implored Father Longtin to help her, but he simply pointed to the sky, his eyes wide. Smokey was running over to help Kay himself, but he too stopped in his tracks and looked up when he realized something strange was happening in the sky above.

As the senator held the Spearhead aloft, thunder began to roll, the ground shook, and the wind roared. Light began to rain down from above as if from a dozen search lights. The children thought the heavens themselves might be opening up—until they saw dark figures falling from the sky.

The senator and his henchman were equally confused. What had seemed like a moment of victory was now turning into a nightmare as chaos whirled around them and the army of dark figures continued to fall from the sky.

In a moment it suddenly became clear what was happening. The thundering sound was the *chop-chop-chop* of a helicopter. The FBI had arrived.

"Agent Nighthawk, FBI!" A man landed behind the senator and snatched the Spearhead out of his hands. Another agent landed beside him and slapped a pair of handcuffs on the senator.

Agent Nighthawk said, "Senator, you're under arrest."

The senator's henchman let go of Kay and tried to run into the woods, but within seconds, the whole clearing was ringed with federal agents clad in black gear.

"Where do you think you're going, pal?" asked one of the agents. The senator's henchman stopped cold in his tracks. He looked around for some means of escape but saw none. Realizing there was no way out, he held up his hands and surrendered.

"What is the meaning of this?" the senator screamed as he tried to wriggle free of the handcuffs. "Do you know who I am?"

"Yes sir," Agent Nighthawk replied. "We know who you are,

and we also know you were behind the robbery the other night at the American History Museum."

"I have no idea what you're talking about," the senator complained. "I want to speak with my lawyer!"

"Take them away," Agent Nighthawk said. His colleagues quickly led the senator and his henchman off to an FBI boat that was docking beside the senator's speedboat. As Agent Nighthawk turned away from the senator, he looked at the Spearhead in wonder.

"Steven, I thought you'd never get here." Father Longtin approached Agent Nighthawk, and the men shook hands.

"Sorry, George, it took us a little longer to get these choppers into the air than I would've liked," Agent Nighthawk replied.

"You know each other?" Marci asked, still clutching Father Longtin's back tightly.

"We certainly do," Father Longtin replied. "Children, this is Special Agent Steven Nighthawk. He's a member of your tribe and an old friend of mine."

"Nice to meet you, children," Agent Nighthawk said. "You're Archie and Kay Mahood, aren't you?"

"Uh, yes, we are," Kay replied. "How did you know?"

"Your mom and I go way back," he replied with a smile.

Mrs. Mahood had been a Secret Service agent for years, so it wasn't too strange that she and Agent Nighthawk might have known each other. Even so, it was strange that he would recognize Kay and Archie, since they had certainly never seen him before.

"We're sorry for all the trouble we've caused," Archie said, "but I promise it was for a good reason!"

"Why are you children after the Spearhead?" Agent Nighthawk asked.

Father Longtin set Marci down on a nearby log while they told Agent Nighthawk the story of Hector's accident and explained that they were searching for the Spearhead to save his life. Agent Nighthawk listened intently and nodded sympathetically.

"I'm awfully sorry to hear that about Hector," he said. "Is he still in the hospital?"

"Yes, that's why we're hoping to use the Spearhead," Marci replied.

"It's the only thing that can save him," Kay added.

"I wish I could help, children," Agent Nighthawk replied, "but the Spearhead is meant to be used to heal members of the Patawomeck Tribe. I don't see how it will be of any use to Hector."

"Please, Agent Nighthawk," Marci said. "We've got to try."

"I'm happy to give you an escort to the hospital, but you should prepare yourselves for the likelihood that the Spearhead won't be able to help Hector."

"You are a remarkable group of children," Father Longtin said. "You should be very proud of yourselves for accomplishing all that you have, but you must also understand that Agent Nighthawk knows what he's talking about. I would suggest that you take Agent Nighthawk up on his offer to escort you to Alexandria Hospital so you can be with Hector. His fate is in God's hands now."

He then turned to Agent Nighthawk and said, "Steven, I'd love to join you, but I'm afraid I have to return a speed boat, or I'm going to have one angry high school crew team on my hands."

"I understand," Agent Nighthawk said with a laugh as he

reached out to hug Father Longtin. "It was good to see you again, old friend."

"Likewise," Father Longtin said, returning the embrace. Then, turning to the children, he said, "Thank you for allowing me to be a part of your adventure this evening. You're a special group of children, and I promise to keep you and Hector in my prayers."

"Thanks for all your help," Marci replied with sullen eyes. "We couldn't have gotten this far without you."

With those words, Father Longtin turned and headed back toward the beach where he had left the speed boat. He returned a few moments later with Marci's wheelchair, which they had left behind. Then, as he walked back to the boat, a familiar, thunderous noise approached overhead.

"There's our ride, kids," Agent Nighthawk said, pointing to the helicopter that was descending into the clearing. "Are you ready to go see Hector and your parents?"

18

Normally, a flight over Alexandria in an FBI helicopter would have been cause for excitement. Unfortunately, Marci, Kay, and Archie were not experiencing the ride under normal circumstances. As they zoomed over the lights of their hometown, the children were somber. Even Smokey was whimpering, and it wasn't because he had never flown before. It was sinking in that, even if they had saved the Spearhead, they had likely failed in their quest to save Hector. Now they could only hope that some other miracle would intervene to save him, but deep down, they knew that wasn't likely to happen.

Agent Nighthawk had radioed ahead to the hospital to alert them that he and the children would be arriving. When they landed on the tarmac, a nurse was waiting to escort them to Hector's room. Agent Nighthawk told the nurse that Smokey was his K-9 dog, so even Smokey was allowed to enter the hospital.

On the walk to Hector's room, the nurse informed them that the Judge and Dr. Gonzales as well as Mr. and Mrs. Mahood were there. The children grew increasingly nervous as they approached the hospital room. They were excited to see their parents again but also dreading what they might say. After all, the children had disappeared for several days and caused their parents incredible stress. They were sure to be angry.

The children hesitated on the threshold of Hector's room as Agent Nighthawk said, "Folks, I believe I've found some people you've been looking for."

The adults looked up in shock to see their missing children in the doorway. The kids were apprehensive, not quite sure how their parents would react, but they didn't need to wait long. In half a second, their parents were out of their chairs and tearfully embracing them.

"How's Hector?" Marci asked.

The Judge looked at her from behind puffy eyes.

"He's still in a coma," the Judge replied. "It's not good."

While the children were reuniting with their parents, another unexpected reunion took place as well.

"Uncle Steve, is that you?" asked Mrs. Mahood as she finished hugging Archie and Kay.

"It sure is," replied Agent Nighthawk. "How have you been, sweetie?"

"I've been worried sick about these children, but other than that, things have been good." She reached out to hug him.

"Hey, Steve," said Mr. Mahood as he embraced Agent Nighthawk in turn. "How long's it been?"

"Too long," Agent Nighthawk replied.

"Wait a second. Agent Nighthawk is your uncle?" Archie asked his mother.

"Yes, he's your grandpa's little brother," Mrs. Mahood answered.

"So, *our family* is the family that's been protecting the Spearhead all these years?" Kay asked.

Agent Nighthawk nodded.

"How come we've never met you before?" she asked.

"Well, when your grandfather passed away, it fell to me to safeguard the Spearhead," he replied. "Since the Spearhead has been sought by dangerous people—like Senator Maxwell—for centuries, I decided it would be safer to limit contact with my family so my duties didn't put them in danger. But I didn't think my niece and nephew would come looking for the Spearhead with one of their friends someday."

"Neither did we," Mrs. Mahood replied. "We've almost worried ourselves to death over the last few days."

"Well, there was no need to worry," Agent Nighthawk replied. "I've been watching over them ever since the kids got into DC, so they were never in any real danger. This is a special group of kids—they're the first people in over one hundred and fifty years to find the Spearhead."

"They found it?" Mrs. Mahood asked in astonishment. "All three pieces?"

"They sure did—all three pieces. In fact, I have the complete Spearhead right here," he said, taking it out of his pocket.

"Is that the Patawomeck Spearhead?" the Judge asked.

"Yes," Agent Nighthawk replied with a bemused smile. "You've heard of it?"

"Only in legends that my grandfather used to tell me when I was a kid," the Judge replied. "It's real?"

"It most certainly is, and these children have found it," Agent Nighthawk replied. "It's my duty to ensure that the Spearhead doesn't fall into the wrong hands. When I heard there had been a break-in at the Masonic Temple, I suspected it might be some thieves looking for the first piece, which had been hidden there for years since my great-great-grandfather hid it there back when he was Grand Master of the temple. I knew the first piece was being temporarily housed at the Museum of American History with the Valley Forge exhibit, so I decided to stake out the museum. While I was there, I was shocked to find that the thieves I was looking for were actually these three kids."

"I'm sorry, but I'm hopelessly confused," Dr. Gonzales broke in. "What's so special about that rock in your hand?"

Agent Nighthawk briefly explained the history of the Spearhead, including that its healing powers had only ever been used by members of the Patawomeck Tribe.

"So, putting aside all my medical training for a minute, even if the Spearhead has healing properties, they won't work on my son?" Dr. Gonzales asked Agent Nighthawk.

"Correct."

"But I may have a way around that," Archie said.

"What do you mean, son?" Mr. Mahood asked.

"Maybe I could transfer the Spearhead's healing powers on to Hector."

"I don't understand," his father replied.

"I only went blind because I got sick when I was little, right?" said Archie. "Maybe if we try to use the Spearhead to cure my blindness, I can somehow pass its powers on to Hector instead?"

"Oh, honey," Mrs. Mahood said, "that's very thoughtful, but I don't think that's how it works."

"Has anyone ever tried it?" Archie asked.

Mrs. Mahood looked at her uncle, who shrugged.

"What do we have to lose?" Archie asked.

"One thing that I know from the stories passed down through our family is that the Spearhead can only be used on a person once," Agent Nighthawk said. "If you're right about being able to pass its curative powers on to Hector, you won't be able to use the Spearhead a second time to restore your eyesight."

"We can't let you do that, Archie," the Judge said. "If the Spearhead works, its healing powers should stay within your tribe."

"That's okay," Archie replied without hesitation. "I'd rather hear Hector's voice again than see him lying in a hospital bed."

Dr. Gonzales had a hard time believing the stone in Agent Nighthawk's hand could cure her son, but even so, she was grateful for Archie's gesture. "Hector's lucky to have friends like you and Kay."

"So how does this work?" Archie asked.

Agent Nighthawk didn't think Archie's plan would work either, but he stepped forward anyway to begin the healing ceremony. He directed Mrs. Mahood and Kay to stand on one side of Hector's bed, while he and Archie stood on the other. He then placed the Spearhead in Archie's palm and directed the rest of them to hold hands while Archie placed his free hand on Hector's forehead.

"The three of us will pray for the Spearhead to cure you, Archie," Agent Nighthawk said. "Meanwhile, you can pray for its healing powers to pass through you and on to Hector, if that's what you want."

Archie nodded. Agent Nighthawk began chanting in the Patawomecks' native Algonquian language. Nothing happened for a few moments.

But then, to everyone's astonishment except for Agent Nighthawk and Mrs. Mahood, the room was suddenly awash in light coming from the Spearhead in Archie's hand. The light that was emanating from the Spearhead appeared to gather into a mass in the middle of the room and shoot through Archie's dark glasses.

Everyone else closed their eyes for a moment as the brightness of the Spearhead became too much to bear. When they opened their eyes, everything was as it had been before, except for one thing.

"Mom, what was that light?" came Hector's weak voice.

Upon hearing Hector's voice, Smokey leapt into his hospital bed and began furiously licking his face as if it were an ice cream cone.

"Oh my goodness," said the Judge under his breath. He, Dr. Gonzales, and Marci rushed to Hector's bedside with tears in their eyes.

"Why are you crying?" Hector asked his family between giggles at Smokey's manic face-licking. "And what are we doing in this room?"

After a momentary outburst of emotion and joy at hearing Hector's voice, Dr. Gonzales sprang into action, putting aside the role of mother and assuming the role of doctor.

"How do you feel, sweetie?" she asked. "Does your head hurt?"

"I'm okay," Hector answered. "Nothing hurts at all. I'm just a little tired. I feel like I've been asleep for a week."

Dr. Gonzales methodically checked Hector's pulse and vital signs before removing her stethoscope and staring in befuddlement at her oldest child.

"Hector's as healthy as can be," Dr. Gonzales said to her husband. "It's as if nothing ever happened to him."

The Judge looked at Archie and the Spearhead he was still holding in his palm. He embraced the boy.

"I don't know how we can ever thank you," he said.

"It was nothing," Archie said.

Mr. Mahood rushed to his son and, grasping his head, asked, "Your eyes—can you see?"

"No, but it's okay," he replied. "Being able to hear Hector again was all I wanted."

"So, what will you do with the Spearhead now?" the Judge asked Mrs. Mahood and Agent Nighthawk.

"Our family will go on protecting it," Mrs. Mahood replied. "I guess we'll just need to figure out where to hide it now that the secret is out."

"Well, if you ever need any help protecting the Spearhead," Marci said, "you can always count on me."

"Speaking of that, I think we'd all like to hear about the adventure that led you to the Spearhead," the Judge said.

"On one condition," Marci replied.

"What's that?" the Judge said, crossing his arms and arching his eyebrows.

"You have to promise not to ground us," Marci said.

The Judge laughed as he hugged Marci. "Since your little adventure saved your brother's life, I'd say that's one condition I can grant."

The kids were starving, so they had the hospital send some food up. Then they spent the next hour telling the adults and Hector all the details of how they had come to possess the Spearhead. The story was almost too fantastic to be true, but after what they had all just witnessed, the adults and Hector believed every word.

"I can't believe you guys had the best adventure ever, and I missed the whole thing!" Hector exclaimed.

Everyone laughed, and as they retold the story, Kay, Archie, and Marci—not to mention Smokey—realized Hector was right: it was by far the greatest adventure they had ever had. They had no way of knowing that it certainly would not be their last.

Aknowledgments

Many thanks to my family, who inspired this story and are always my first editors. Thanks also to Christina Kann and everyone else at Brandylane Publishers/Belle Isle Books whose hard work and insight vastly improved this book. My gratitude also to the Patawomeck Tribe of Virginia, whose history breathes life into this fictional story and who, along with a nonprofit for those with special needs, will receive donated shares of the author's proceeds from this book.

About the Author

JOHN ROCHE is a native of Alexandria, Virginia, where he still lives with his wife and four daughters. When he's not driving his daughters to soccer and softball games or writing adventure stories for children, he works as a lawyer in Northern Virginia and Washington, DC.